Devils' Hill

Nan Chauncy

DEVILS' HILL

Illustrated by
GERALDINE SPENCE

FRANKLIN WATTS, INC.
575 LEXINGTON AVENUE, NEW YORK 22, N.Y.

For
VERYAN LOVEDAY IN ENGLAND
and
NICKOLAS BRUCE IN AUSTRALIA

Contents

Glossary

billy	*billycan: a real Australian word for a tin bucket with a lid; used over an open fire*
cobber	*chum*
crook	*ill, ailing*
to create	*to make a fuss*
damper	*bread made of flour-and-water, American cowboy-style, and cooked in ashes of campfire*
dial	*face*
fair cow*	*annoying, bad*
flaming	*cursed*
to fossick	*to rummage about, to explore*
gallah	*fool, stupid one*
natter, nattering	*chatter, chattering*
nipper	*small child*
'roo	*kangeroo*
sookie	*unweaned calf; also feeble, soft, sissy*
tarn	*small mountain lake*
tucker	*food*
veges	*vegetables*

* It is said that only an Australian can call a dark horse a "fair cow" and be understood!

Devils' Hill

1

Badge Leaves for School

"Aw, well . . . well, I best get going," Badge muttered reluctantly, still turning his back on the thin track leading through dense Tasmanian rain forests to the world Outside.

He was Badge Lorenny, going to school for the first time. In all his eleven years he had never seen so much as the outside of a school building.

"I best get going," he repeated, still facing the west—the wrong direction—with eyes fastened on his mother's, like the lost stare of a possum disturbed in daylight. His fingers clutched nervously at the rope round his pack and for several heartbeats neither of them said anything. Then she looked away over his head—his mother was tall and strong—watching Dad load up the pack horses down the track.

Badge was her youngest child and the one she secretly loved the best of her three; he was the last to leave home in search of knowledge. She gave him a quick glance, taking him in from the unruly top of his straight hair to his heavy boots, and paused at the boots.

The hair she had cut herself, and though it stuck up like the teeth of Dad's saw she could do no more with it; nor could she help the long, wistful face beneath—nor the thin shoulders and knobby knees. Boots were different: boots were important.

These particular boots had been passed down from his elder brother Lance. They curled at the toes so, his sister Iggy said, they could "take a good look at Badge's ugly dial"— Iggy always had a back word for everything.

"Boots all right, son?"

"They're good-oh since Dad fixed 'em, Liddle-ma."

It was a family joke of the Lorennys to call their big mother "little," which became "Liddle-ma"; they seldom used the usual bush term "Mum."

Liddle-ma was thick and straight; she had to bend her head every time she stepped through the doorway of their little bark-roofed home.

Badge dropped his gaze to his own feet and the neat patches sewn on his boots by Dad, who patched boots as Liddle-ma did clothes, till there was almost nothing of the original left.

He gazed but saw no boots; an idea which had been smouldering in his mind had burst alight, and he knew suddenly with passionate force he did not want to leave home and live at Uncle Link's farm, nor go to school with his cousin Sam and the rest of them. It would have been different if Iggy had been there, but Iggy had done with country schooling and followed Lance to a wonderful place called "Hobart" where he was told houses had glass windows and beds stood on legs.

Homesick in advance, he swallowed and raised pleading eyes. "Aw, Liddle-ma . . ."

He could say no more. He would have given all he owned in the world—which was in fact a camera given him by an American cousin—if Dad would have set off along the track without him.

Of course his mother knew; she groped for words to comfort him. "There's Sammy, son. Now Iggy's gone, you'll like someone . . . a boy will be better. A boy your own age, like Sam. A big family, like; there's little girls, too, but Sam and you'll play around together. You two boys . . ."

Her voice trailed into silence, but it was quite a speech for Liddle-ma. Badge was also a shy person of few words, and so they stood saying nothing, just staring at each other as mute as a pair of frogmouth owls pretending to be a dead branch.

Dad called back, "Where's the boy? Isn't Badge coming?"

Overhead a flock of mountain parrots clapped their wings and flew squawking to a flowering gum tree. Their chatter broke the stillness of the bush as they ripped to pieces the honey-scented flowers. Liddle-ma gave herself a little shake and said briskly, "Dad's waiting on you, son. Give Auntie Florrie the lettuces. Put on dry socks the minute you get there, and watch the track—it's as greasy as fried mutton birds after all the rain."

Badge nodded dumbly, though he wanted to explain about Sam. He'd met him several times at the Gordon River, going with Dad to help fetch the supplies Uncle Link brought in. He didn't like Sam: Sam made him feel a fool, and that wasn't a right thing to do to a chap who was older by close on half a year. He did it in little ways and he did it in big ways; and once he made Iggy laugh at him, too.

That was when Sam had offered him money, a big

pile of money or one small bit; and laughed fit to bust when he chose the big pennies instead of the one small bit of silver.

No, he didn't like Sam: he laughed like a mountain parrot. The next time, he asked if Badge would rather have a pound of gold or a pound of feathers? Well, a chap whose dad was a prospector knew a bit about gold, so first he said "gold." Then he changed, because he himself saved any pretty feathers he could find and would much rather have feathers than gold.

First Sam said he couldn't change, then he said he could, then he said both answers were wrong, and then Badge hit him on the nose and they had a bit of a fight. He still didn't know what the right answer was, but he'd ask Iggy one day.

"Look, Dad's unhitched Prince. Get going, son."

Badge wanted to say he'd fetch in double the usual firewood, if only he might stay; but instead he turned right round and plodded off towards Dad, treading in all the muddy potholes. He and Iggy always squished through wet holes happily: now he squelched the harmless mud with anger.

He thought of the time he'd found a special green frog by the river, and how Sam had grabbed it and told a lie, saying it had jumped away. No, he didn't want Sam with his tuft of curls like the crest of a black cockatoo.

He thought of Liddle-ma and wondered if she watched him go, or had gone back to get on with the morning's jobs; he couldn't look back to see because Iggy had told him men never looked back after saying good-bye.

Liddle-ma had said "Get going, son"—was that saying good-bye?

Yes, he decided, squishing mud under his boot, it was the same.

4

2

A River in Flood

THE valley which was home and world to Badge was unknown outside the Lorenny family, except to one bushman. Years ago Dad had discovered it by accident when prospecting for gold in the wild south-west of Tasmania. He told only his brother Link, who had a farm near Ouse, and they decided to keep the discovery to themselves: it was their valley.

Dad discovered near it a stretch of good grazing on hills roughly enclosed by low cliffs, due to a fault in the rock formation. This made a wonderful natural fence round a big run for cattle; so they took possession, drove the first cattle in, and Dad made his home in the valley.

Apart from fencing troubles, the greatest difficulty had been cutting a track in and finding a means to cross the Gordon River when in flood—in that wet part of the world the rivers may suddenly become impassable even in summer. But they got round this problem with two stout wires slung from trees.

The track-making had been worst down the steep face of a mountain they called Three Fists which bounded their valley to the east. It was heart-breaking to climb this slippery zig-zag in wet weather, though years of Dad's

5

life had gone in "improving" it. Today as always, he called a halt when the horses reached the top.

"Good on yer, Prince! Good on yer, Di'mond!" he praised the sweating animals. "Take a spell: we on'y works a twelve-hour day out here. Not like city chaps, eh, Badge?"

"Dad," protested his son—after appreciating Dad's small joke—"just now you said somethin' about 'rest for man and beast.' Prince is a horse, not a beast. And I'm not a man, am I?"

"Soon will be, son. Soon will be." Dad gravely fetched out his plug of tobacco and pared it carefully into the leathery palm of his hand. "A bit o' school learning, and in no time . . ."

Flinching from the word "school" Badge walked away abruptly, leaving Dad to his pipe. He didn't want to think of what lay ahead to drag him away from all he knew and loved—his whole world. So he went to the very edge and stood looking over the precipice deep into the valley.

As a rule, though he tried to conceal it from Iggy, Badge hated looking from heights: today he was too absorbed to feel afraid. Down there the sun was gleaming whitely on log fences and dead trees and twinkling on fat, glossy leaves of green. There were greens of all shades; a stranger looking over the valley might have thought them all native to the bush, but Badge could pick out the raspberry patch and the currant bushes, the gray-green of the roof, and the tender greens of the vegetable garden which were so different from the tender green of ferns.

A whiff of strong tobacco made him aware Dad was beside him.

"Watch out you don't slip, son, or you'll reach home

6

quicker than you thought. See that range, yonder?—see the one with jagged rocks atop like broken teeth? You can't see it from home but I was out there one time, prospecting. Them two bit o' white like a rabbit's scut on'y shows up like now, after heavy rain."

"What makes 'em, Dad?"

"Water splashing down the rock. Could be a tarn on top there, I never got up to see, I had to turn back. Where I looked acrost was an ole native devil scratching himself in the sun, so I called it Devils' Hill. There was a valley between, but I didn't get down to it. Might have had good feed," he ruminated; "could be cattle country. We ought to take a look out there one day, you and me, son."

For an instant Badge's face brightened, then it closed down sullenly as he muttered, "I won't be here. I'll be at school."

Dad turned and knocked out his pipe on a boulder. "You won't if we stand nattering any longer. Uncle Link and Sammy will have given over waiting at the Wire and gone back to the Farm." Then, noticing the gleam in his son's eye, he added, "And that would mean no lift in the Land Rover, son, only another long walk after the Wire."

Badge moved away, saying nothing.

"Gid-dup!" said Dad. Prince and Diamond lurched forward.

It was steamy-hot when they left the bald heads of the ranges for the deep, wet valleys. Badge stripped to the waist, but that old bushman Dad would do no more than unfasten the top button of his gray flannel shirt, saying, "Better be hot than et alive by 'squitoes and ticks and leeches, son."

7

There were plenty of trees down after the recent gales, and rushing streams where no creeks had been before. Sometimes even Dad stood perplexed, and Badge was sure they were "bushed," for the axe cuts blazed on trees were there no more, the trees themselves having gone.

But Dad just stood a moment scratching his chin with his thumbnail before pointing to a wall of greenery and saying, "The track goes through there, son."

"Can't we go round it, Dad?"

"Maybe, but I'm leaving nothing till next time. If you got to cut a tree, cut it whiles it's green. Fetch the axes; and best put your shirt back on, there's a leech having a free beer on your shoulder, son."

It seemed unending, but at last they came in sight of the biggest river, the Gordon, which should have been shallow enough to ford at this season and was in fact a raging torrent. Tree trunks were spinning down the center like matches.

"There's been a lot of wet down here," Dad shouted against the thunderous roar, "let's hope the Wire's not broke."

They left the horses under the usual wild cherry and hurried to the gap where they could see across. The wires, one above the other, still held; though the bigger tree trunks seemed almost to touch the lower strand.

It was a mighty stream. In the middle great brown bubbles whirled by so fast Badge could not hold them with his eye; tangled spars and broken ti-tree replaced the greenery of the banks, and all was devastation. But Dad looked only at his Wire, his Bridge, his Road to his brother's farm and the world Outside.

"Not too bad a flood," he smiled proudly, finding his Wire intact.

"But Dad, Unk and Sam—they're not here?"

"No, but the Wire's all right," said Dad.

3

Crossing the Wire

THE Wire was all right, still intact, and Dad unperturbed; but Badge gazed at it fearfully, for it seemed a mere spider's web dangling low above the racing, raging water. The thought of crossing with a pack on his back made him gulp suddenly and look down, and his eye fell on a pile of glistening, yellow-brown foam.

"Spongy toffee!" he said aloud. (It didn't matter what you said, the roar carried the words away unless you shouted.) Spongy toffee was the name Iggy had given to the lovely, insubstantial stuff. Had she been there he knew they would have been risking their lives to rake big lumps ashore with long sticks. Would Sam . . . ? But Sam was not there.

"Look at that snag," Dad shouted in his ear, pointing out a jam of logs up-stream. "Nip and fetch the rope off of Prince, son, and I'll work it free."

The rope fetched, Dad made it into a lasso and got to work. He told Badge not to wait but to hurry across to the little clearing where Uncle Link parked the Land Rover, and say he was coming.

Badge reached the Wire but he did not hurry across. The crossing looked terrible to a tired boy, and anyhow it was fun to stand by the tree and watch Dad's efforts. His first fling missed the log: his second also caught nothing, but Dad himself overbalanced and had to step knee-deep in water to recover himself.

A wide grin spread over his son's face as he watched, entranced. Unluckily Dad glanced up and saw the grin. "Get on over!" he bellowed. "You get over before I come to you!"

Hastily Badge grabbed the top wire and stepped on the lower. With hand sliding to hand above, and boot to boot below, he dragged along sideways, trying not to think of the fury of brown water boiling up under his boots.

As he neared the middle, the swaying wires dipped lower with his weight and the pack pulled him backwards till he saw the whole giddy whirl coming up to meet him . . . but he righted himself in time, gulped down sick fear, and hauled himself over the worst place. He hoped Sam was not watching for he had his eyes shut tight as he dragged the rest of the way to the tree on the bank.

With his back to the river—which partly deafened him—he stood among ferns trying to master a spasm of dry retching. He did not know Dad was there until he heard, "Good on you, son! It weren't too sweet a crossing after all."

From Dad this was praise indeed; his shoulders straightened as he followed him along the twists of a path they kept concealed and overgrown. It broke suddenly into the clearing where Uncle Link was busy loading lengths of green lumber. "Hullo, Unk!" he shouted. "Where's Sam?"

His uncle stopped work to watch them come, indicating he wasn't the man to strain his voice shouting against the roar of the Gordon. Like Dad, he wore a gray shirt without a collar, neatly fastened at the throat with a gilt stud; his trousers were greeny-black with age and held up by a thin strap of leather, into which his old pipe was thrust like a dagger. His lean face, crinkled as an old leaf,

was quick to smile, and though he might look at you gravely there was always a twinkle at the back of his eyes. Instead of answering Badge's question he bestowed on his nephew a big wink.

"Well, Link, how's things?" Dad asked as he dropped his pack.

"Not too wonderful, Dave. Florrie's been crook again."

Badge perceived they were about to start an endless, boring nattering about Auntie Florrie's ill health, and what Iggy called "the noos of the day about a year old."

"Didn't Sam come?" he inquired hastily.

"Sammy's not home, he's been down in the city some weeks now, he wasn't to come home till school started. How did you enjoy crossing the ole Gordon in flood, son?" he twinkled.

Badge thought of Sam and how he would have answered this one, his curly head held cockily as when he boasted of the big loads he carried over the Wire. He dropped his pack and swaggered forward imitating Sam. "Aw, not too bad, Unk. Could've been worse. I made it all right."

"So I see. I'm real glad you had fun getting over the Wire, Badge, for now you can turn and go back again."

"Go back?" his nephew gasped, thinking if this was one of Unk's jokes it was a very bad one. The very mention of the Wire made it rise before his eyes, swaying and dipping horribly so that already he felt dizzy.

"That's it. Some boys is born lucky: you can turn for home again after you've had a spell."

"What's all this, Link?" Dad asked as he pared tobacco.

"No school on Monday. Whooping cough. School's closed and we're keeping ours away from the other kids. I wish Sam could stay where he is in the city, but they can't keep him there forever. It's a fair cow for Florrie having all the kids on her hands when they ought to be at school."

Badge's voice broke in harshly. "Meaning I don't have to go to school yet awhile, Dad?"

"You heard what your uncle said, son." Dad stuffed his pipe thoughtfully and there was a long silence: Dad

14

was thinking. He lit a match, got his pipe going, blew out the match, stamped it in the ground, and turned to his brother. "Come to that," he said, "if Sam had come along today, maybe we could have taken him out home for a week or two? One less for Florrie to look after. But seeing as he isn't here . . ."

Uncle Link slapped his thigh. "Would you take him next full moon, Dave, when we come in with supplies? Would you?—if we haven't got whoops, and we'll know by then? My word, it'd be a help and I bet young Badge would be glad of a cobber."

Badge said nothing. He'd told Liddle-ma he didn't want Sam and nor he did; yet . . . he'd like to go with him to the river now and see who could rake in the biggest pile of spongy toffee. Also Sam out home might be different from Sam skiting at the Wire. But would Dad really let him come and see where they lived?

As if answering his thought, Uncle Link said, "Sam won't let on where he's been, Dave, I'll see to that. Any road he's got sense underneath, Sammy has. I know he's a bit full of himself just now—see, the boy don't get much chance at home, his Mum fusses over him too much all the time, and there's too much gap between him and the next: he bosses Bron about, being a girl; and the twins are just babies, and Sulvie not much more. He'll be right enough with another boy of his own age."

As if repenting his rash offer, Dad said, "As to that, Badge don't look for any mate till the holidays, when Iggy's home. Do you, son?"

But Badge astonished him—and himself still more—with a fervent, "Aw, Dad, I'd like Sam to come out home."

15

"Would you, now?" Dad scratched his chin gently with his thumbnail and looked at his brother. "Then that's settled, Link—if none of them go sick. What about a bit of tucker?"

They rested in deep content, backs propped against a fallen tree, eating magnificent sandwiches from the Farm of cold lamb spread with pickles or tomato sauce.

Like music the distant river sang in Badge's ears—he was going home! (The crossing was nothing if you faced towards home.) The full moon, which might help them home tonight, would grow little and weak and another moon be born, and this one grow from a thin, bent sapling of a moon to one as round as a sawn log before he need think of school again.

By then Sam might be along . . . yes, old Sam might be all right on his own, out home.

4

Calamity

LIDDLE-MA took the news calmly.

"Poor Florrie," she said at breakfast, "we must help her if we can. Twin baby boys are handful enough for a sick woman and then there's Sulvie, on'y about five. What's *she* like, Dave?"

"Last time I was at the Farm she was like one of them small ponies with hair over its eyes. A real card. Had a bit of a hammer and was bashing nails in a board. Every time she missed the nail and bashed her finger instead she said, surprised-like, ' 'T'urts!' But she never stopped, she went right on bashing: *bash*—' 'T'urts!' . . . *bash*—' 'T'urts!' You never saw such a trick!"

"She sounds a rum 'un. What about Bron?"

"I reckon Bron's the rouse-about to the lot o' them, you never see her without she's in a fuss. Looks frightened of her own shadder. Thin like a rock lizard and darts about just the same as one."

"I can see Sammy'll be glad to get with another boy." She smiled across at Badge who sat cramming toast into his mouth and listening to every word. It was news that Sam would be pleased to come, and he would have said so only his mouth was too full. He began to wish the old

17

moon would hurry up and die and let the new one take over—the new one that would bring Sam.

"When I saw him last, Sam promised to be tall like his dad," Liddle-ma went on, "with blue eyes and dark curly hair. He had a ready smile, too; I don't wonder he was Florrie's white-headed boy."

"Aw, Liddle-ma," protested Badge. "His hair couldn't be both?"

"It's a manner of speaking, son," Dad explained. "Liddle-ma means his Mum thinks the sun rises and sets over him, which she still does, seemingly." He passed his mug for more tea and added, "He's well set up for his age, bigger and better covered than Badge, here."

"But I'm older," Badge informed him quickly.

Liddle-ma glanced at him shrewdly through the steam from the billy. "That's right, son, you're older, and he can't take that from you, can he?" she said.

It was strange, but now Badge was not so contented with home as before he went to the Wire. He was always trying to see it with Sam's eyes. They had meat every day Outside, Iggy said, not only when Dad killed a beast or snared a 'roo; they had fruit, and there was no fruit now the raspberries and strawberries were finished. Cream on the table saved butter-making on the Farm, Dad had told him; but Liddle-ma used the cream to make all the butter she could; she salted it away for winter when their best friend would be gone, their friend being good Old Bow'ra the cow; each winter she went to the farm to have her calf and when she returned it was spring indeed.

Certainly there was Narrups the pony which they could ride in turns, but where would they ride to? Would Sam enjoy what Badge loved most, going deep

18

in the bush where only Dad had been before, finding hidden pools or rocky clefts which even Dad had never seen?

"What's up, son, staring like a snake at a bird?"

"Nothing, Dad. I were just thinking."

"Then think this firewood inside to Liddle-ma before it rains."

Every day they expected rain but only a few showers came in the mornings; Dad said the big storms which had flooded the Gordon must have used up the usual supplies of wet.

The nights were fine and clear, filled with still beauty and the occasional weird cry of owls wailing for "More-pork! More-pork!"—and once the snarling cough of a Tasmanian devil hunting far away in the hills.

Each night after the evening meal Badge slipped outside to study the moon, for the Lorennys had no calendar with dates he could cross out with a pencil. The old moon lost shape like ice thawing in the bottom of a bucket, and soon bedtime came before it rose at all.

It was while the early night was still dark that something happened when he was asleep, an event that cast a deep shadow.

He had been dreaming he and Sam were hunting for frogs with silver stars on them when all the frogs roared like thunder and became Dad calling through the wall, "Big tree down, son! Like to come and see?"

Half asleep he fumbled his feet into boots, pulled some clothes on, and followed Dad into the cool night air.

"Why did it come down when there's no wind?" he asked.

"Beats me! The storms a few weeks back may have

loosened the roots, but—a night like this . . . " Dad shook his head at the great stars above and the wide, peaceful world. "Got your cat's eyes? Good, then we won't need a lantern. Come on."

He set off with great strides, making for the southeast. Once he paused for Badge to catch up and said, "It fell somewheres near the paddock where we puts Old Bow'ra."

"Aw, it might take the fence?"

"It might take more'n the fence," Dad answered grimly.

They smelt the fragrant scent of the eucalypt before they saw the hump of its back and the gap where it had stood. Several smaller trees had come down with it.

"It got the fence all right," Dad said as they paused to stare, "but it's come clean across and filled the hole with itself. Could be worse, son."

But it couldn't have been worse, for they found it had got Old Bow'ra, too. She was not killed, but a branch had struck the shed where she slept and she was pinned beneath it.

"Can you find the way back to fetch the axe, son?" Dad asked urgently, as he tried in vain to move the branch away. "I reckon I can take some weight off of her till you come. Tell Liddle-ma."

Old Bow'ra was moaning softly as he sped away, and he was not ashamed to cry a little as he ran, thinking of her lying there. Bow'ra, who was one of them: the best cow that ever was! He remembered, too, that her last heifer calf had got away as a yearling and gone bush— Dad thought a snake might have got her. Anyhow there would never be another Bow'ra. Oh, she *mustn't* die!

"I knew!" cried Liddle-ma, when he stumbled home.

20

"All of a sudden I knew it was poor Old Bow'ra . . . I was coming along," and he saw she was ready dressed. They fetched the axe and food, and dipped water for her in a bucket as they passed the creek.

Dad's face looked queer and white in the starlight: he was crouched under the great bough on hands and knees, taking some of the weight from their cow.

"You shouldn't, Dave . . . it's too much," cried Liddle-ma.

"Cut some . . . limbs off . . . whiles I hold it," he ordered between gasps.

Badge fancied himself with an axe but his mother was quicker; so he tried to help Dad with the weight instead, crawling under the bough and wincing each time a blow fell trembling through the green wood, making poor Bow'ra moan so pitifully.

When Dad took the axe she was soon free and made efforts to get up, but when they got her on her legs she seemed to have no strength for standing.

"Maybe—a drink?"

Badge fetched the bucket and put it under her nose while she was still supported. They were delighted when she not only drank, but managed to lick a little bran from the bag as well.

"Aw, Dad, if she eats she must be right," said Badge as they settled her comfortably on the ground again.

"We'll just have to see, son. She'll be right where she is till morning; there'll be no milking, of course, but we'll come over early to see how she's doing. Best get a wink of sleep now."

"If there's no milk, what'll I feed Ticcy on?" Badge asked. Ticcy was his latest pet, a baby ringtail possum which had fallen from a high tree—Dad thought a hawk had got the mother. Already he had taught it to lick jam and lap fresh milk with its tiny tongue—at present it ate nothing else.

Liddle-ma's voice sounded strangely harsh as she answered, "It won't be only Ticcy goes short if our Bow'ra . . . " She turned away without finishing.

As they went home a waxing moon stuck a gold horn over the top of a black hill.

5

Hoof Marks

WHEN Badge woke, the sun had just cleared the knobs on Three Fists and there was no one at home, breakfast lay uncleared on the table, and porridge was cooked on the hob.

When he had eaten and washed up, he went to Ticcy's box with milk from the previous day in a tin lid. Ticcy uncurled himself from a warm nest and rushed up his arm and round his neck and down again to lap eagerly at the milk.

"Ow, your liddle claws do tickle!" Badge told him. "Good job you like that milk, it's the best I can do. Try eating the bit o' damper under the jam, you fussy ole party, and I'll fetch you some young peppermint-gum leaves to chew."

He was just leaving for Old Bow'ra's paddock when he saw his parents returning and yelled, "How is she? How's the ole lady?" In the morning sunshine nothing seemed as bad as at night and he was sure by now the faithful Bow'ra would have recovered.

"Not too good," Dad called briefly. "Come and help get the wood sledge. We're going to haul her home where we can look after her better."

They got out the biggest sledge, a simple affair made of the fork of a tree. Dad spent some time lashing bars across while Badge and his mother stuffed bags with bracken, arranging them on top where the cow would lie.

"Will I fetch Prince now?" Badge asked when all seemed ready.

"No, son. We got to fix the place where she's to go, first."

Close to the back of the house was a stout bar between two trees where Dad hung sacks of meat after he had killed a beast. Above this he now rigged a roof of bark for shelter, and hung a padded sling from the bar.

"What's that for, Dad?"

"To take the weight off of her legs, son. I don't rightly know what's wrong, but she'll do better this way."

Liddle-ma stuck her head through the window-opening to see the sun. "It's getting late," she called. "We best have our dinner before we goes to get her."

A melancholy procession left the paddock late in the afternoon, for there had been endless difficulty getting Bow'ra on top of the sledge, the sledge through the slip-rails which were too narrow an opening, and finally in getting the sledge itself pulled along. Prince alone could not do it; Diamond had to be fetched as well.

Dad led the team, Badge and his mother hanging on behind to prevent the whole thing running away down an incline. Dusk was falling as they reached the shelter and, tired as they were, they had to throw all their weight on the rope which lifted Bow'ra inch by inch from the ground.

At long last she was suspended to Dad's satisfaction, with her hoofs resting on the earth but taking none of her weight.

"Will I put Prince away now?" sighed Badge, longing to rest himself.

"Yeah, she'll do now if we gives her a feed."

They watched her tongue lick round the dainties in the old zinc tub and told each other she would be all right, now.

"Hurry and fix the horses," said Liddle-ma, "tea's waiting on you."

Badge hurried, but when he got in he felt too tired to eat. He gulped some tea and went to bed.

He was just closing his eyes when he heard Dad say through the wall, "If you keeps an eye on Old Bow'ra, mate, the boy and me will get at the big tree in the morning. I want to cut it up whiles it's green and sledge it in for winter firewood."

"Can't it wait till Sammy's here to take a turn?" his mother suggested. Badge lifted his head, listening eagerly for Dad's reply.

"No, it can't; that's more'n a week away and the greener it is the easier the job will be."

Badge's head thumped down again. More than a week to wait for Sam, and then . . . and then it wasn't certain-sure he'd come!

"Wait on, son! Take a-holt of the saw more like I do," Dad called from his end of the log. "Don't put your weight on it, just draw back steady . . . like so . . . again . . . see?"

25

Aa-ar—zarr-rr! rasped the monotonous saw, again and again till time had no meaning.

"Wait, son!" called Dad again from his end. "Let her come gentle, let her come sweet. No call to pull yer insides out."

Aa-ar—zarr-rr! rasped the saw once more. Again and again, world without end.

Badge was hating Dad up there, chanting away his, "Press even—and pull! Press even and *pull!*" while the saw went forward and back. There was no longer morning or afternoon, sunshine or breeze, only that back-breaking old rasp, *Aa-ar—zarr-rr!*

At last a pause: "Don't let her jam, son! Keep at it, keep the saw straight." And once more the everlasting *Aa-ar—zarr-rr!*

But suddenly Dad shouted, "Look out, she's through! Yank out the saw, quick!"

The vast trunk quivered and groaned but it was not quite ready to break apart. Again Badge gripped the wooden handle with hands slippery from sweat.

"Let her be!" Dad called, mopping his face. "She's as near as your nose and I'll finish her off with the axe."

Badge stood up and looked round while the world wheeled back into place. He discovered it was a fine, sunny afternoon and time to brew the billy of tea. How many afternoons had they spent already cutting up this old tree?

"Will I bring the sledge along after we've had tea?" He liked this job for it meant a ride out behind Prince.

Dad considered the question as he tipped sugar in the mugs. "No, son. I reckon we'll give over for today," he said at last. "I'll bring the wedges and split her up before sledging it in. Best give the horses a spell now, seeing the

moon's almost at the full and we'll be taking them to the Wire in a couple o' days."

Badge smiled, propping his back against his enemy, a length of tree trunk: life had suddenly become good.

"Are you wishing you'd gone to school last moon, after all?" Dad asked with twinkling eyes. "I worked you hard, didn't I, son?"

But his son shook his head happily, for it was over now —the back-breaking toil, the futile anger against Dad, the fury of having to keep time with the saw—over at least for the day. Instead was a rich thankfulness, a deep pride.

"I don't reckon Sam could mince up this ole tree with a cross-cut saw?" he suggested shyly.

"Shall we bring him and let him try?" Dad laughed. "Shall we give him a go?"

They did not leave at once, for everything must be stacked tidily and Badge was making a great pile of the green leaves in the middle of the paddock.

"Once it's rained enough to be safe from bush fires," Dad had said, "we'll set a light to it one night and have a bonfire." This, it was understood, would be to entertain Sam, who might never have seen such a blaze, nor smelt the glorious scent of green gum leaves roasting in millions, popping and crackling like fireworks, and screaming in the heat.

Badge was just dragging in a leafy bough to add to the pile, when Dad called excitedly from the spot where they had taken Old Bow'ra through the slip rails, "Come here, son! Come quick!"

"Snake?" he called back, looking for a suitable stick, for Dad was peering at the ground.

"No, no! It's . . . come and see." He was on his knees now.

When Badge came blundering along in his big boots he was told sharply to mind where he trod. "It's tracks, son—and don't you tread on one of 'em! Tracks like Bow'ra's going in and coming out—on'y poor ole girl, she's been slung up for more'n a week so it can't be her. Look!"

Badge looked in awe. "Cattle got out?" he suggested.

"I'll have to see if they've found a gap, but if one gets out it's mostly a lot o' them, one following a leader. Them single tracks going in . . . going out again . . . by gum, I shouldn't wonder if——"

"If what, Dad?"

"Best not make a wild guess till we see what your Mum makes of 'em."

"Aw—Dad!"

"Come on, we'll go and fetch her now."

6

When One Moon Wanes

THEY did not reach home till the sun was low and glorious pinks and reds spreading over the western sky, and Liddle-ma was not there; nor was she with Old Bow'ra.

Badge found her at last in a far corner of the vegetable garden filling a bucket with ripe tomatoes.

"It's good you've come, son," she said as she straightened her back. "This spell o' fine weather's ripened them a treat. We got to keep them picked down for fear an early frost gets them."

Badge looked at them with distaste, though their colors rivalled the sunset sky. "Ticcy don't eat termarters," he said.

"Look, son, I gave you that tin o' powdered milk for Ticcy—and it means we do without ourselves till the supplies come in. It's not Ticcy's food I'm worrying about, it's ours."

"We had termarters for breakfast; we got to have 'em again for tea?"

"We got to, and be thankful. Without Old Bow'ra's milk I dunno how I'm going to manage, and your dad out all day on the wood-cutting and no time to fetch in a

29

'roo. You can dig a few spuds while you're here," she added, pointing to the potato fork stuck in the ground.

"Aw, Liddle-ma, we seen something, Dad and me. We wants you to come and take a look." And he told her about the tracks.

Liddle-ma actually paused in her work, she was so interested. "It could be, son, but too late to go and look tonight, the sun's setting already."

"What 'could be,' Liddle-ma? Dad wouldn't say. Tell us!"

"If it's small hoofs like Old Bow'ra's . . . remember the heifer she had, the one that got away when the men was driving her back to the Farm? A brindle she was." His mother went on softly as if talking to herself. "Brindles are always good milkers. I said a little prayer just now . . . I said, if the old moon passes away, I said, there's a new one. I don't like asking, I said, but if she goes (and she don't look to be getting better) it could be downright awkward—with young Sammy coming, too . . ."

"Won't Sam eat spuds and termarters? Don't he have to, at home?" asked Badge eagerly.

His mother looked at him as though surprised to see him still there, and said, "You trot in with that green stuff for Old Bow'ra, son. Tell Dad I'll be along soon."

They sat later than usual round the fire after tea, planning things out. Dad said: "Bear in mind the moon's near the full: on'y two days left before we goes to the Wire."

"I know that," said Liddle-ma. "If we want to use the pack horses it's got to be tomorrow, so's they can rest up the day after. Well, you and me better get off early, Dave

30

—take a look at those tracks on the way out, and ride on round the cattle run to see if there's a gap anywheres."

"I could go on Narrups, he don't have to rest up?"

"No, Badge, we got to leave you to look after Old Bow'ra. It wouldn't be right for us all to go and the poor thing maybe feeling bad and looking for comp'ny."

"And who said we wouldn't take the pony?" Dad asked. "Aren't we expecting to fetch back young feller-me-lad Samuel?"

So in the morning Badge was left in charge of the place, while his parents rode a way towards the sun that was just showing above the top of Three Fists.

He let Ticcy out while he washed up and tidied round, and as the little creature climbed the back of Dad's barrel chair he told it all the news.

"See, Ticcy, there's on'y today and tomorrer, and then we go to the Wire for Sam. Oh, I know! I know Sam may have the whoops and not show up. I know that. But there's on'y today and tomorrer to go if he *is* there, see?"

He gave Ticcy his food on the table while he cleaned out the box and fetched fresh leaves for him, then shut him in carefully and went to have a look at Old Bow'ra.

She hung dejectedly as usual with her bones making angles under the rug of sacks they had sewn for her, her head lowered into the tin bath of food. Badge thought it was a funny thing he hadn't noticed before how her haunch bones stuck out.

"Look, ole girl," he protested, "you didn't ought to look so poor, seeing you never stops eating."

He stood watching her miserably; he had never doubted before that she would get well as long as she stuffed in food, but now he remembered Dad saying, "She seems to get no good of her tucker."

Certainly all this eating had left her very thin; perhaps it was too dry and she needed something green and juicy? The thought sent him speeding away to hunt for sow-thistles and choice tit-bits from the garden.

She looked much the same when he returned, but she had stopped eating and when he tipped the green stuff in the bath she only stared at it vacantly.

"Water? Is it water you want?"

He fetched a fresh bucketful from the creek; she leaned

over as if smelling it, groaned slightly, and did not touch a drop.

"Look, Bow'ra, I don't know what you want, and I wish Dad was here. Is the band too tight under your belly?"

Climbing on to an old crate he pulled the rope Dad had fastened and managed—so much weight had she lost—to lower it a little. In the end he was sorry he meddled, for she only slumped down and he could not manage to tighten it again on his own.

He was growing distracted: every time she breathed now, she moaned softly. "I can't do no more, can I?" he demanded, tears in his eyes. "You won't eat, you won't drink, and you won't stand on your hoofs. Oh, *how* I wish they'd come home!"

The day dragged by and she certainly did not improve. Badge fetched her their Sunday cabbage from the garden and she would not even sniff it.

"Just one leaf?" he begged. "You got to get strong, you got to eat, Bow'ra. You don't want to drop your bundle, do you?"

He put the cabbage in the house and ran down the track to see if they were coming. He had done this already half a dozen times, though he knew it was too early to expect them. He had to do something to get away from the sound of Old Bow'ra in pain, and this time—he could hardly believe it—Dad and Liddle-ma came riding round the bend.

"Aw, Dad!" he gulped. "It's Old Bow'ra! She's been groaning and carrying on and she won't look at a cabbage."

Dad dismounted from Prince and gave his son the reins: he looked very sorrowful. "You two go on and put

33

the nags away," he said. "We can't have Old Bow'ra in pain."

The stable of slabs and bark was some way from home: Badge did not say a word till they were inside and then he asked, "What can Dad do for her, Liddle-ma?"

Liddle-ma looked at him and was about to speak when the valley's most frightening thing happened, the report of a gun echoing round the hills.

"That's all we can do for poor Old Bow'ra now, son," said his mother gently.

Next day Badge fetched the two big horses to hitch once more into the sledge and they dragged Old Bow'ra's body back into the paddock where she had spent so many hours contentedly chewing the cud.

Dad raked carefully round the bonfire Badge had built and when they had hoisted her into the middle of it, put a match to the leaves.

The fire roared and sang, the green gum screamed as it burned, the flames stretched up to the sky, while the three of them ran round with wet sacks, putting out the sparks where they set light to tussocks of grass or whorls of bark.

At last the fire died down to a great red furnace and Badge snatched the half-burned sticks and threw them back on top.

By dusk it was low enough to leave safely. "But we'll come and have another look before we goes to bed," Dad promised.

As they walked through the slip-rail gap Liddle-ma pointed to the ground. "The sledge has wiped out the tracks," she said.

"Aw, that's bad. Did you see 'em first?"

34

It seemed a long time since Badge had seen his mother smile, but she smiled now. "I saw 'em, son, and I don't need 'em again. Yesterday, Dad and me saw what made 'em, didn't we, Dad?"

"That's right, Badge, and no gap in the cattle run—the fence round good enough to keep a young heifer from joining the mob inside."

"So she came looking for her mother, maybe? Hanging around, likely as not, son, when we fetched Old Bow'ra home. Hung round this very paddock."

"Was she here when you seen her, then?"

"Not far away, grazing. She's gone wild, of course, after all this time, and when we come, she was off at a gallop. But not before I see she was Brindle."

"She was Brindle all right," said Dad, "and we got to get her, *somehow*." He sighed. "I'd be off after her to-morrow if it wasn't for going to the Wire. I'd rather follow her while the tracks are fresh."

Badge gazed round at the bare peaks and green valleys and the far lonely ranges and wondered, "How you going to catch her, Dad? What's to stop her if she just keeps going, like?"

"If we could round her back in this paddock . . . ?" Liddle-ma looked back a trifle hopelessly. "Oh!" she said and pointed suddenly to a great moon lifting over the hill.

They stood a moment to watch it rise.

"Time we was home," said Dad. "Got to turn out early tomorrow, son."

So much had happened, Badge was almost forgetting —*tomorrow Sam would come!*

35

7

A New Type of Dog

FOR once Badge was awake before Dad's voice had boomed through the thin partition of his lean-to bedroom. Today Sam would come—he must come, then there would be things to do together instead of forever pulling on a saw or thinking of poor Old Bow'ra.

Of course Sam would be different here where he'd never been before; maybe he'd not always liked him at the Gordon crossing but when Sam saw what it was like out home—well, he'd be different. Badge was quite certain about that.

So he astonished Dad by jumping from his fern mattress on the floor at the first call, and was out fetching the pack horses before the sun was up.

Three Fists was in shadow as they climbed the Zig-Zag to the top but the track was not so slippery as before, since there had been unusually little rain lately. They came into dazzling sunshine up above and the world seemed new and sparkling.

"Whoa, there, Prince! Whoa, there, Di'mond!" Dad cried, calling the usual halt. He sat on a rock to prepare tobacco for his pipe and Badge perched beside him. He was not interested today in looking down on home, he was thinking about something else.

"Dad!"

"Yes, son?"

"Dad, if you was asked which you'd rather have, which was the most heavy, like, a pound of gold or a pound of feathers—which would you choose?"

"Which I'd like to have is one thing, son, which is most heavy—that's another. Try giving me the gold!"

"But gold's the wrong answer. So's feathers." Badge's forehead was wrinkled with the problem. "Sam said so!"

"Look at it this way. Say you was to load Prince with a pound of this or a pound of that, would he care?"

"Not so long as—aw! By gum, Dad, I see it! Whatever I said was wrong *because the weight's the same!* Sam fair tricked me, didn't he?" Badge beamed up at his father. "Now I got to trick him back."

They sat in silence, Dad puffing contentedly and the horses swishing flies. A wedgetail eagle circled and swooped in the blue above and Badge followed it with his eyes, though his thoughts were absent.

37

Suddenly he smiled. "I got it, Dad! Say you stood one side of a river with a pound of gold and a pound of feathers and chucked 'em both across, which would get to the other side first?"

"The gold, for the feathers might all blow back in your face, son."

"Wrong, Dad! See, the feathers would be *on a bird* what would fly across. Good-oh, that'll trick Sam!"

"You seem counting a lot on young Sammy showing up," Dad remarked as he knocked out his pipe. Badge made no answer in words but he sprang up and set off eagerly along the track.

Their first glimpse of the Gordon showed a respectable river keeping within its banks, instead of a raging monster. As usual they left the horses in the shade of a wild cherry and hurried to the Wire.

"I don't see Unk about. Will I shout?"

"Best nip over—likely he's there but didn't hear us coming. You can give a shout if you like whiles I fetch another load down."

So Badge yelled, "You there, Sam?" and bounced on the Wire, hauling himself over in half the usual time. As he stepped off under the big tree he saw someone was waiting for him. Yes, it was Sam!

"Good on yer, Sam!" he cried eagerly, his face one huge grin.

Sam did not respond, his face was scowling: it looked to Badge like a thunder cloud spreading over a sunny sky, and he wondered what he had said wrong.

"What's up, c-cobber?" he stammered, taking a hesitating step nearer.

Sam's lip curled and his tone expressed the utmost disgust as he jerked a thumb behind him. *"This,"* he stated,

38

and for the first time Badge noticed someone peeping at him from round Sam's elbow.

With open mouth he stared at a thin, pale girl with frightened gray eyes . . . He was just placing her as a timid, flustered little wren, when he saw her birdlike claw of a hand clutching a short, dumpy child whose hair came over her eyes like a bird's nest. There was nothing frightened about this one; through the fringe of brown hair her black, beady eyes glinted wickedly at his, as if enjoying his gaping surprise.

The thin girl began to speak in a quick, flustered squeak. "I'm Bron. This is Soolvie, she's the youngest excepting for the twins."

"*Not,*" contradicted the young lady calmly.

"Oh, yes, dear—you are, Soolvie. That's your name, isn't it, Sam?"

"*Not!*" repeated the child, her eyes still glinting at Badge, as if this was some private joke between them. Sam looked into the distance, pretending he hadn't heard.

"She is Soolvie only she won't have the name," Bron explained distressfully. "She likes to be called something else, but Mum——"

"*Sheppie,*" stated the child so firmly that somehow that settled the matter. Bron fastened her scared eyes on Badge again. "You're Badge, aren't you? D'you think your Dad'll have us? Mum told Sam he couldn't come without we came, too. Mum said——" she broke off, her fingers moving nervously.

"That's right, they would mess things up for me," muttered Sam, still scowling and looking ashamed. "Not my fault, Badge."

A warm glow shot through Badge: so Sam had wanted to come!

"I couldn't help it, could I?" whined Bron. "I

39

didn't——" she checked abruptly: Dad was crossing over
the Wire. At the same time Badge could hear Uncle Link
whistling as he pushed his way towards them through the
ferns. He reached them first and greeted his nephew with
the usual great wink, waving them all back as he strode
on towards his brother.

40

The two men leaned on the Wire talking earnestly, their tones too low to be heard properly by the group of silent children watching them. They saw Uncle Link gradually become excited, running his rough hand through his mop of graying hair, and a few words came to them.

". . . you don't know what it's been like, Dave! . . . What else could I do? . . . Got to go down . . . operate on her, maybe . . . Can't leave three kids on their own."

Dad listened quietly, saying little and scratching his chin thoughtfully with his thumbnail. Then he looked up and saw the listening group, muttered something to his brother, and came over.

"Well, Bron? And how's this one, how's Soolvie?"

"Not!" came the answer, but with the twinkle of the eye for Dad.

"She means not to call her that, Dave, the kid's gone crazy over horses and dogs lately. There's an old English sheepdog—you know the breed, hair all over the eyes—goes by the name of Sheppie——"

"Sheppie!" beamed his younger daughter.

"No matter how her Mum does her hair, she gets it back over her eyes, don't you, Soolvie? Like that dog."

"Sheppie," she corrected him gently.

"Come on, Dave, the boys can tote the stuff across whiles we exchange the noos of the day back by the car."

The men vanished along the ferny track while Badge found three pairs of eyes watching him, waiting for him to speak. He swallowed and looked at Sam. Sam scowled back.

Badge couldn't think of a thing to say but at least he made the attempt. He felt the whole world was listening.

41

"Aw, well . . ." said Badge breaking the silence at last. That was all. No further words came out.

Sam had plenty to say. Ignoring his sisters' feelings he explained bitterly how they had been hung round his neck like a drag-chain, because of his mother's illness and the school being closed.

"I couldn't help it," whined Bron. "It wasn't my fault, Sam. Nor I don't want to come out here all amongst the snakes and things." She looked down at the river and shuddered.

Badge found his tongue at last, "Snakes is mostly minding their own business, Bron, and more scared of you than what you is of them."

"Bron's scared of everything," said Sam.

Bron raised her shrill voice in plaintive protest but Badge was watching Sheppie. This little girl interested him enormously; he strongly approved of her name and of choosing it for herself. Hadn't he exchanged "Brian" for "Badge" long ago, after Iggy had complained, "Brian tags after me like a young badger following its mother around"? Hadn't Liddle-ma answered, "Maybe he does, for he's a faithful little wombat, aren't you, Brian?" Then Iggy had said, "I shall call him Badger," in her teasing voice; but he'd liked the idea of being a Faithful Badger and the name stuck like a bidgee burr.

Sheppie had left Bron: she was stooping down and peering across the river through her hair. He noticed from the back her ears stuck out and curved forward rather like Ticcy's. Never having seen a dog, he thought with her black eyes she should have called herself a possum instead—but of course it was for her to choose.

"Look at that kid," Sam's voice cut in, "she'll be down in the river in a minute."

42

" 'Orses!" said Sheppie, pointing with a short, rather grubby forefinger.

"Aw, she's seen Prince and Di'mond eating their tucker over there," Badge explained.

Sheppie turned slowly round and looked at him through her hair. "Sheppie go to 'orses," she coaxed in her funny, deep tones.

"She crazy, she can't get over the Wire without Dad—you got to see she don't try," Sam told Bron fiercely.

" 'Orses," repeated Sheppie sweetly.

"Me? Ow! I can't stop her, Sam! You know if she's set on a thing she gets it in the end," wailed Bron.

Sheppie seemed to turn this statement over with interest, and her eyes slid to the two wires, the top one suspended far above her reach. While Bron and Sam argued, she came and stood close to Badge. "Take Sheppie over?" she suggested.

"Don't you do anything of the sort!" shouted Sam. "It's just a try-on. Don't take any notice of her, Badge, unless to give her a clip over the ear."

For a moment Sheppie studied Badge's face, then with a sudden movement she grabbed his leather belt and held it tightly. "Take Sheppie!" she commanded.

"Smack her hand—hard!" cried Sam, rushing forward.

Badge shook his head indignantly, Bron squeaked she'd tell her Dad on Sam, and the outcome of the confusion was Sheppie standing calmly with her other hand as tight round Sam's belt as a creeper round a stump.

Sam blustered and smacked but the small hand would not let go. In the end he gave way and the two boys slid sideways across the Wire taking very small steps. Between them a small child swayed, coupled to their belts, while Bron was left fussing and snivelling on the bank behind.

8

Dad Takes the Risk

No sooner had Sheppie got her feet on the other bank than she ran to the horses, crawled beneath Prince and sat down under his belly to watch him eat.

"He'll kick! He'll trample you flat, and serve you right!" shouted Sam. But Prince seemed not to notice; he munched away steadily at the bran in the bag on the ground.

"Prince won't hurt her," said Badge. "If she'd gone to Di'mond, now . . . well, Di'mond bites."

"What say I stay and keep an eye on her, while you tote a load over the Wire?"

"Aw, Sam! Couldn't we both go together? Sheppie's all right there."

But Sam was suddenly feeling very responsible for his sister and Badge returned alone. He found Bron dancing about like a wild thing with its leg in a trap, squealing she could never, never cross the river on that bit of wire.

Badge considered the problem. "You could swim," he suggested, "it's not real deep now."

It seemed Bron couldn't swim for fear of snakes, but she must get across to mind Sheppie—"for you know what Sam is at looking after her, no more use than a wet Sunday," she explained; and there, sure enough, they could see Sam down by the water taking off his boots to cool his feet, leaving Sheppie neglected.

"I could get you over, Bron," he offered shyly. "Put your left hand on the wire so I can put my right on top and sort of *haul* you along, see?"

It was odd, but he found himself explaining away and helping Bron over just as though he had never himself been sick with fright at the crossing. Her hair, he noticed, though untidy, was fine and soft as fur, and her whole face seemed to come to a point at her nose—just like a bandicoot's. Perhaps after all Bron was more like a flustered little bandicoot working hard for its family, than a small chirpy wren?

She was much more trouble than Sheppie. About the middle, where the wire dipped lowest, he could feel her shaking with fright and making strange possum noises in her nose. He clutched her hand tight and hauled her along, but she nearly fell off at the end when a sudden yell startled them. It was Uncle Link following them.

"Hoi! Where you kids going to?—what you done with Soolvie?"

Badge shouted explanations back and pointed to the native cherry tree. He heard Dad laugh and say, "What did I tell you, Link? They can get across if they want to."

Sam hastily scrambled back to his post and soon they were all gathered round Prince, watching her father's efforts to dislodge Sheppie.

"You come on out of it, now!"

"Don't want."

"If I have to pull you out you'll be sorry."

He stooped down, but Sheppie with a quick wriggle moved away and wrapped herself round a foreleg where

she clung like a leech. Prince chewed away unconcerned.

"Prince seems to have taken to her," said Dad thoughtfully, "and Bron, she's got herself across the Wire. Look, Link, I reckon after all I'll take the risk."

"Wouldn't have asked you if I'd knowed about Ole Bow'ra."

"I know that. But seeing they're here . . . Plenty spuds and tomatoes so they won't starve for a month."

"As to that, I killed a pig. There's your share in the pack." Uncle Link broke off to address his daughter sternly. "But Soolvie won't go riding anywhere on Prince, she won't go out to your place, Dave, seeing she can't do what she's told."

Sheppie removed herself from Prince's leg and ignoring her father, stood before her uncle, a wicked black eye glinting at him through her hair.

"Take Sheppie!" she implored.

"Not without you do what you're told all times. Out my place kids do what they're told, don't they, Badge? You got to understand that, Sheppie," said Dad.

The child beamed and nodded vigorously—he had called her Sheppie!

The loads were carried across the Wire in record speed, Sam showing off to Badge how much he could tote, Badge showing off to Bron and Sheppie how little he was afraid of swinging over on the swaying contraption.

The two girls sat on the bank below dabbling their feet in the cool water. Badge had provided Bron with a fine whippy stick and shown her just how to kill a snake with it, while Sam laughed and said she'd be dead with fright before she would use it.

When all the loads were over and Bron had boiled the billy for them, they had a fine feast of cold roast chops brought from the Farm, and laughed at Sheppie who gnawed her bone pretending to be a dog.

"Like to come with me and fetch Narrups?" Badge asked Sam, for he had left his pony apart from the pack horses under a different tree.

Sam looked at the men busy now with the balancing of loads, and at Bron putting out the fire and tidying up after the meal, and nodded.

"Take Sheppie!" came a low, husky demand. Sheppie

had not known there was another, smaller, horse. She tried to stumble after Sam on her short legs, tripped in the undergrowth, and fell. She did not cry when Bron fetched her back but waited tensely, watching where the boys had disappeared. When the fat, white pony with flowing mane and tail appeared, she stared as though seeing a vision. "For Sheppie!" she breathed as though stating a simple fact.

Sam was indignant. "Well, I like that! Badge brought it today for me to ride—he just told me so, didn't you, Badge?"

"Aw . . ." Badge flushed, noticing tears of disappointment welling in the dark eyes. "See, Sam, I didn't know then about Bron and Sheppie. I—I reckon we best take turns?"

"Not me," Bron said hastily, "you can have my turn, Sammy."

"Huh!" Sam turned away in disgust. "Wish I'd brought my bike."

"Why, Sam, you haven't got a bike?"

"Not at home I haven't, Bron, but at Mrs. Jolly's where I was in the city——"

"And if you had, you couldn't ride it out here. Could he, Badge?" asked the practical sister.

"You shut up, young Bron, and don't shove your oar in where it's not wanted. I'm not talking to girls, I'm talking to Badge. You——"

"You spare your breath for climbing the hills, Sam," advised his father coming up behind them, "and take the billy and tie it on Di'mond's pack. Time we was off. Who's to have first go riding the pony? Who's it to be, eh, Badge?"

"Aw . . ." his nephew mumbled distressfully, know-

ing Sam was listening and had paused, ready to turn back:
yet seeing Bron's imploring gaze also—not for herself but
for Sheppie; and seeing two black eyes through hair willing him . . . willing him . . . "I reckon it better be the
littlest, don't you, Unk?"

"Thass right, son."

He swung the dumpy child on the sack which served
as a saddle. She pressed her knees tight and sat still, radi-
ant with joy.

9

A New Life Begins

IT was a long, weary journey home. Dark had gathered in the bowl of the valley when at last Badge looked down from the top of Three Fists, and the moon had not yet risen.

He wanted to point out a friendly gleam down there in the great dark space, a red glow which would be lamplight or firelight shining through the red bit of cloth Liddle-ma had drawn across the window-hole to keep out moths. It was also her signal of welcome to the weary ones trudging in from the Wire.

But Sam had slumped down where the horses stopped; and Bron, half-asleep herself and forgetting to be scared of snakes, ants, and other perils, sat with her back to a log with the sleeping Sheppie in her arms. Only Dad strolled over while the horses rested.

"She's coming to meet us, son." He pointed out a tiny, flickering light like a match, saying it was the lantern Liddle-ma carried. They watched it dance a little nearer, not speaking their thoughts, which happened to be the same, each anxiously wondering how Liddle-ma would take the arrival of three instead of the one extra mouth to feed, of more eyes to see inside their valley.

"My turn now to ride Narrups," Sam announced with satisfaction, when they returned.

"Your luck's gone walk-abouts, Sammy," Dad said. "No one rides down the Zig-Zag without they want to arrive in the valley on their head. Prince and Di'mond goes first, then the pony. You can hang on to his tail if you like."

"Gosh, no! He might kick."

Dad smiled and went to start the laden horses: it was left to the shocked Badge to explain that whatever mean thing the pony might do he never kicked and was trained for tail-hanging.

Sam listened. His silence said, "If I believe everything I won't believe that," and he let Narrups walk away past him.

"Well, Bron," Dad said as he swung Sheppie on his back and made her clasp her hands round his neck, "would you like to take a-holt of the tail, or of my pocket?"

Bron stared fearfully into the yawning black hole down which the horses were disappearing in single file. There were endless things to be afraid about and most of all the dark, but her uncle was not one of them. She stretched out a timid hand and grasped his bluey coat.

"You boys go in front of us. I reckon Sammy's wishing he'd brought that bicycle contrapshyon he was telling us about, to ride down the hill?"

Sam scowled as he plunged after Badge down the steep Zig-Zag, which was a water course in wet weather and full of loose boulders. He was beginning to think he didn't like his uncle.

Liddle-ma was waiting for them where the track forked, one path leading to the stables. She held the lantern high and watched them come. They dodged in and out of a stand of blue gum saplings where the track emerged

51

from the Zig-Zag, so she had plenty of time to grasp what had happened.

The two big horses came first; they trudged up to her and stopped; they knew Dad would unload certain things before Badge undid the slip-rails and led them away to supper. Badge came next, with a hand twisting hold of Narrups's tail, and Sam behind him. Liddle-ma looked away over their heads and met Dad's eye. They must have talked without words, for she called cheerfully, "Why, Sam, I'm pleased to see you, son, and glad you brought your sisters along."

"Mum's sick, that's why, Auntie."

"She may go to the hospital," Bron added, staring with anxious eyes, wondering about her welcome.

"I reckon she'll soon be right with you all away and a bit o' peace and quiet," Dad said. "Young Douglas is with friends and there's only the twins left to plague her. This" —as he carefully parted two small hands and set her on the ground—"this calls herself 'Sheppie,' so we'll call her that out home, will we?"

"Thass right." Liddle-ma watched the small girl blinking at the lantern while loading something unasked on her back. Then she held out her large friendly hands, saying, "Come on, Bron, come on, Sheppie! We'll go on in and make the tea for them, will we?"

Sam stood uncertainly, looking first at Dad unloading and Badge pulling out the rails which made a gate, then at the great black void all round him and the bright gleam of light from a window up the slope. He turned to follow Liddle-ma.

"Wait on, Sam," called Dad, who must have had eyes at the back of his head, "aren't you forgetting to carry your load, son?"

"Bron didn't!" snapped Sam, his voice harsh from weariness.

"If you was a girl, and Bron was your big brother I wouldn't ask it of you . . . best take this meat and give it to Liddle-ma."

When Sam had gone and Dad was helping Badge with the horses, the boy looked at him wonderingly. "She didn't create one mite, did she, Dad?"

"Liddle-ma?" Dad smiled with understanding. "See, son, Liddle-ma don't hold with hollerin' once the tree's hit the roof. Once before, you remember, she tried to stop your Uncle Link bringing strangers in, but seeing this was only Bron, and her little sister——"

"But she reckoned Sam was another mouth to feed, with Ole Bow'ra gone?"

"That's so, but whining about it won't turn back the Gordon in flood, will it? Nor make the porridge go farther. Come on, son, we'll cut an armload o' bracken after tea to make two extra beds."

The table was festive when they got in; it had clean newspapers for a cloth and no less than three candles stuck in bottles spaced down the middle, while the walls reflected an orange glow from the huge fire. Sheppie, mounted on a pile of coats on an up-ended log, clasped a steaming mug of soup while her black eyes darted round, gleaming with satisfaction.

Bron, too, seemed very much at home; she crouched by the fire making toast on a pointed stick while she chattered to Liddle-ma. Only Sam seemed ill at ease.

"Tired, Sam? You sit up and make a start, we're ready, now."

53

"I'm all right, Auntie. Don't you have any light but candles?"

"We keep the kerosene for the lamps and have to go careful with it, don't we, Dad?"

"No fun packing-out lamp oil, son."

Liddle-ma stood ready with a great ladle in her hand. "Bring the bowls, Badge, and you and Bron can set them one at each place as I fill them. Sam will finish making the toast for Bron, won't you, Sam?"

"At Mrs. Jolly's where I was in the city," said Sam to no one in particular, "they had a machine that made the toast on both sides and turned itself off so it couldn't burn."

"Aw . . . ?" said Badge politely.

"Look out, Sam, you're burning that bit," Liddle-ma pointed out. "Seems you'll have to carry that machine you spoke of round with you." Badge gave a gulp of laughter which he stifled quickly at the sight of Sam's scowling face.

For a time there was no conversation, everyone being too busy eating the good, thick soup, and spreading the crackling slabs of toast with butter and jam or slices of ripe tomato.

One by one the knives were laid aside and mugs of chipped enamel, filled with sweet, milkless tea, replaced them; the fire-lit room was filled with drowsiness and peace.

"What's that noise outside?" cried Bron suddenly, her voice sharp with fear. There was a strange little hoarse cry and an impatient scratching on wood close by her.

"Aw, that's not outside, that's Ticcy in his box over your head, Bron." Badge got up and moved round the table.

"Where? Where?" she screeched, moving away so fast

54

she knocked the up-ended log which served as a chair crashing to the floor.

Everyone sat up, startled. Sheppie, who had been drifting into sleep, turned round and stared at the box above her, dimly seen in the shadows of the corner. Something thin and whippy dangled down from the wire netting in front. She pointed with her stubby finger. "A '*nake!*" she announced, much interested.

"Take it away! Take it away!" screamed Bron, colliding into Badge and dodging behind Liddle-ma for protection.

"Aw, Bron! That's not a snake—it's Ticcy. Look, I'll show you, he on'y wants his tea."

"You're mad, Bron, course it's not a snake," said Sam, relaxing, yet still keeping his eyes fixed on the dangling, twitching thing that was so snakelike.

"Ticcy's a pet possum," Liddle-ma told Bron, placing a large, comforting arm round her shoulders. "Badge found him lying stunned-like, fallen from a high tree."

"That's his tail sticking out," Dad explained. "See the white ring of fur near the end? That's how you tell he's not a brush possum but a ringtail."

Several pairs of eyes followed Badge's movements, watching him open the front of the box. Then they saw the wondering black eyes, the wide ears, and the soft, gray, furry little body as Ticcy shot out and ran up an arm, pausing to look down from Badge's shoulder.

"Give Sheppie!" implored the little girl, stretching out her arms.

"All right, you hold him, Sheppie, whiles I gets his tucker. He won't bite, but his claws scratch if you don't watch out."

Sheppie hugged the tiny possum in her arms and stroked him, inviting Bron to do the same. But Bron shook her

55

head after glancing nervously at his claws. "I'm helping Badge fix his tea," she said, tipping some dried milk in half a mug of warm water and busily whisking it up with a fork.

Badge looked round, beaming at the interest being taken in his pet. By all but Sam. "Look, Sam," he offered, "you can feed him for me, if you like?"

Sam left the table, where Liddle-ma was gathering the plates and dishes, and stood by the fire. "No thanks," he said, "I don't go much on possums. Where's the radio? Must be time for the serial."

Dad lowered the newspaper he was about to read: it was months old although it had only been fetched that day, and Dad would not allow it to be a cover for the table until he had read it all. He looked at his nephew over the top. "We don't have one o' them contrapshyons out here, Sam."

"You don't have a radio! But Uncle Dave, what do you do? You don't have lights, you don't have a radio—what do you do when it gets dark?"

"We goes to bed, son."

10

The Harmless Dragon

B ADGE woke as usual with a pale gleam of daylight
coming through the cracks in the shutters over the
window-hole. He got up from his bed of ferns on the
floor to open them and flood the little room with light.
He hoped this would rouse Sam, rolled in his blankets as
dead with sleep as a wombat on a winter's morning.

"That's right, son," said Liddle-ma, sticking her head
through the door, "roust Sammy up. You boys must pick

57

me some more tomatoes for breakfast, we finished the lot last night."

It was all very well, but Sam refused to be roused—or anyhow to get up from his snug nest of blankets. He hugged them tight while he argued with Badge.

"Who wants tomatoes? I don't. I'm sick of the sight of them."

"See, Sam, we has 'em fried for breakfast. Come on!"

"*I* don't. Those who eat 'em can pick 'em—fair go!"

"Look," Badge urged, speaking low so that his voice wouldn't be heard through the wall, "she said—Liddle-ma said—you had to!"

"What's it worth?"

"Worth? What you mean, Sam?"

"A tanner? A bob? What's she give you for picking the flaming things? If it's two bob a time and we go whacks I might help you. Show us the size of the basket."

"Badge!" came Liddle-ma's voice through the wall, "get going! I'm waiting for them tomatoes to fry!"

" 'Get going, Badge,' " grinned Sam as he settled down again. "I knew she wouldn't mean me. I'm the visitor." He closed his eyes.

Badge slipped out, bewildered, and pondered as his cold fingers searched for ripe fruit on the dew-wet plants. Wasn't Sam going to share the work as well as the play? Bron did; he had seen her as he passed, in a colored apron, putting plates round the table. And what could he do to make Sam like it out home?

"That's right," said Liddle-ma, taking the basket from his hands at the door, "the fat's all hot. Where's Sam?"

"He's coming."

Evidently Sam heard this through the wall; he was out of bed when Badge went into the room to persuade

58

him to get up. Badge smiled shyly and jerked his head towards the sound of breakfast turmoil; Sam answered with half a grin and made a face in the direction of his Aunt's voice, and Badge went out happy. Sam was all right.

But it was not so good at the breakfast table. Liddle-ma put before him a large plate of hot tomatoes on toast and Sam passed it on. "That's for you, Sam," she said.

"Thanks, Auntie, but I don't eat tomatoes." He shot a sly glance of triumph at his cousin.

"You et 'em last night," Liddle-ma stated. Everyone stopped talking and stared at Sam; Bron giggled nervously and screwed a corner of her apron in her fingers. But Sam seemed quite at his ease. "Oh, last night," he said.

"Yes, last night!" she told him crisply.

"I'd rather have some ham for breakfast," stated Sam coolly.

"Would you now?" Dad cooed as mild as a bronze-wing pigeon in a wild cherry tree while he showered pepper on his plate. "Rather have ham, eh?"

"That's right." Sam smiled across pleasantly, pleased with his success. Badge sat with his mouth open, still and anxious: it was clear Sam didn't understand Dad.

"So would I, and I reckon so would we all," explained Dad gently, "but it's termarters or nothing. See, Sam?"

"My dad killed a pig, didn't he?" Sam's face was flushed as he glared across at Dad. "You can't do me out of a share, seeing he gave you half of it. Mum said she'd cooked the ham and if I didn't like the sort of—the sort of food you people eat out in the wilds here, I didn't have to eat it for she'd cooked the ham. She knows I like ham."

59

Never in his life—not even when his big brother got arguing—had Badge heard anyone talk back like that to Dad, but Dad treated it as though no one had spoken. Was it because Sam was a visitor? Liddle-ma, too, was eating away and smiling at Sheppie, whose eyes were peeping at her through neatly brushed hair. Sam was looking perplexed. He stared at the sheet of newspaper in front of him and waited.

"Well?" he asked at last. "Don't I get anything to eat in this joint?"

"There's still a bit left in the pan if you're quick," Liddle-ma pointed to the hearth with her spoon. "No, Bron, Sam can get it for himself, you get on with your breakfast."

"I don't eat that stuff." He paused, but the remark seemed to provoke no one. "Mum wouldn't ask me to. Would she, Bron?"

Bron's pale face grew pink with distress; before she managed to answer, Liddle-ma started talking about the weather, just as though Sam had never spoken.

"Wouldn't be surprised if it broke today and we got a good rain, Dave. I hope so, the veges are drying up a treat."

"It feels to me more like thunder. Lucky we fetched in the stuff yesterday whiles it was dry."

Muttering something, Sam scrambled out from the bench and clattered through the door. He would have slammed it behind him only it was a door that stuck halfway and wouldn't slam.

Badge half rose, but a gesture from Liddle-ma made him sit again.

Sheppie showed a clean plate, beamed at herself, and said, "Want Ticcy!"

"Wait. When we've all finished," said Liddle-ma.

"How would it be," she went on, "if you let Bron and Sheppie feed Ticcy this morning, Badge?"

He nodded thankfully and bolted in search of Sam.

Dad had been right about the weather: by the time they had finished the midday meal the day was oppressive with heat and the dome of a black cloud was rolling up from the west.

"If you boys want a swim in the pool down the river, you best nip along now," said Dad.

"That's right, and look out for snakes. Bron will help me clear up, won't you, Bron?"

"Aw, thanks, Bron!" said Badge, eagerly stepping off the veranda into the sunshine. Sam followed him reluctantly.

"What's up, Sam?" Badge asked as he waited for him. "Don't you want to come?"

"Not much. All that way in the heat to step in a puddle. At Mrs. Jolly's where I was in the city we only had to get on a bus and we could step off almost on the beach at Sandy Bay—and that was *sea*. I'm going as far as those trees and then I'm going to sit down for a bit. You can do what you like."

"Aw . . . but Dad'll think——"

"I couldn't care less what your Dad thinks. Nor your Mum neither," he scowled, looking for a place to stretch where there were no ants.

"Aw, Sam! It's good-oh down by the river. We could fish for some of them little trout, maybe, or some yabbis? D'you like fishing?"

"D'you call dangling a lump of meat on a string for a

yabbi *fishing?* Why, at Mrs. Jolly's where I was in the city——"

"But, look Sam, there's things down there . . . platypus . . . colored rocks you can break off and draw with . . . the nest of a pink robin—ever seen a pink robin?"

It was no use. Sam had found himself a nice shady spot and was kicking loose stones aside. "You go on if you want, Badge," he said. "You'll find me here."

"I reckon you et too much dinner—that's what it is!"

"You *shud-up!* I wish I'd never set eyes on this dump out here or anyone in it. I wish—*ow!*" he yelled suddenly. "Look out, there's a blood-sucker! Nearly put my hand on it! Quick, where's a stick?"

Badge had one in his hand and jumped to the attack, looking everywhere for the snake. "Where is it? I can't see it, Sam?"

"There!" He jumped as if to stamp on it, but Badge could see no snake, only a little gray-brown, dragon-like lizard; he waited with the stick poised as its bandy legs carried it round a stone.

"Ow, you're missing it!" wailed Sam. "Here, give us the stick. I saw it go round that stone."

"That weren't no snake, Sam!"

"You ole gallah, I never said it was a snake. Those blood-suckers can bite worse—didn't you know that? If they grab your finger you're for it."

But Badge had thrown the stick aside and grabbed the scuttling little creature in his hand. "These are all right, Sam. Some calls 'em Adelaide dragons, but for all they look so fierce they can't hurt you. Here, take a-holt and see for yourself what friendly little chaps they can be."

62

"Put it down!" yelled Sam. Turning he made a dash through the trees towards home.

Dad, racing to see what was the matter, met Sam who was pursued by Badge holding something in his hand.

"It's a blood-sucker, Uncle Dave! Make him put it down and tread on it! It'll kill anyone it bites!"

Dad took it from Badge and made it run up his bare arm. "Go on—bite me!" he said. "Here's a boy with his head crammed full o' city nonsense about you. Bite me and show him!"

A sound like empty kerosene tins rumbling on a sledge made Badge look at the sky. The black cloud was stealing up to swallow the sun and a hot wind fanned their faces.

"It's coming—run for it!" ordered Dad. "I'll bring this little fellow along to show Bron and Sheppie, so they'll never be scared of a little harmless liz."

A few drops plopped down from the black sky but Badge did not quicken his pace. He was thinking. It seemed after all Sam didn't know everything.

63

11

A Desperate Decision

THE only thing Sam seemed to enjoy those first few days was the thunderstorm. He stood on the veranda with Badge saying, "Gee whiz! that was a beaut!" every time lightning jagged across the black sky in a dazzling flash, or "Listen to the band!" as thunder growled like the dog of a great giant sent to gobble up the mountains.

"Mrs. Jolly (where I was in the city) knew a chap struck down dead by lightning like that flash, when he went to cross the road," Sam went on with relish, after a specially fine streak had lit up the whole sky. "If I were your dad I wouldn't walk about out there." His eyes were watching Dad bringing in a huge log: they were shining with the excitement of a crowd who wait for the accident to happen.

"Aw . . . he's all right, it's not raining more'n a couple o' drops."

"Ah, that's just it. Where I was in the city, at Mrs. Jolly's, they said it was when there wasn't much rain the lightning was most dangerous. Ow, that was a beaut! Wonder where Bron's got to? Hiding under the bed, most likely. She goes stark, staring crazy if there's a bit of thunder about. Girls are like that; you don't know 'em, Badge."

"Well, I don't see how she could hide under our beds, seeing they're on the floor, Sam. And anyways I can hear her inside. Liddle-ma's showing her how to make scones."

A minute later the door opened and Bron appeared with Sheppie. "Look, Badge," she said breathlessly, "Sheppie's made you a man out of dough. She wants you to eat it."

Badge glowed with pleasure as he took the squat, half-baked shape, gray from much handling, from the beaming Sheppie. It seemed wonderful that she had made her dough-man specially for him. But it was at Bron he looked as he said, "Aw, aren't you skeered to come out here?"

Bron winced at a blinding flash, followed by a crackle and thunder, but she shook her head bravely. "Auntie Liddle-ma says thunder don't eat you and lightning don't go round looking for people to strike down dead—like Sam said. She says what you got to do, you got to wait for a flash and then count slow like this: 'One—two—three—four'—see? each number you count is a mile before the thunder hollers."

"Well, what about it?" Sam demanded sourly.

"Then you know how many miles away the storm is, and if it's coming closer or not. *There!*" she cried as another flash lit the sky. "*One—two*—come on, Sheppie! *Three . . .*"

So they stood staring into the blackness, waiting and listening for the first rumble as they counted, only Badge noticing that Bron was screwing the corner of her apron between terrified fingers.

"*Fifteen!*" yelled Sam, as thunder boomed away over Three Fists. "At least fifteen miles away."

"I reckon it's moving round without us getting much rain," said Badge. "We'll count the next one and see, will we, Sam?"

"I must go in and see to my scones," said Bron in proud haste. "Come on, Sheppie—unless you want to stay?"

Sheppie shook her head, she was bored with their thunderstorm; she sidled up to Badge and touched the dough-man dangling from his finger and thumb by one leg, and croaked, "Give Sheppie?"

Sam hooted; Bron looked shocked and said, "Oh, you don't take back a gift, Sheppie!"

But Badge understood. "Thass right, you have him now. I've took off the tip of his boot to eat—see, Sheppie?"

She clutched her treasure back again. She wasn't pleased about the missing bit from his foot either, and went inside to ask Liddle-ma to mend it for her, and to give her another currant for the button missing from his coat. Then she ate the currant, for after all his coat seemed all right without it.

The weather grew unsettled with cool gusts of wind, but the thunderstorm had certainly missed them.

"I don't reckon it was ever closer nor ten miles," Badge said at breakfast one morning. "Remember when we counted, Sam?"

"I know it was never more than ten drops on the garden," said Liddle-ma. "You boys'll have to fetch some from the crik, if no more water falls from the sky. Else what'll we do for pumpkins this winter?"

"I don't like pumpkin," Sam informed them. No one

66

seemed very interested. Sam's breakfast was raw tomato sliced on bread and dripping: he had explained to Liddle-ma that it was only cooked tomatoes he didn't eat.

"Before it gets hot again," said Dad, "we got to fetch some of that wood in from Old Bow'ra's paddock. You boys, when you've watered the pumpkins, can hitch Prince

to the sledge and take it out there for a load. You'll find me up there." He pointed, and left the table in search of his axe.

"Nothing to do in this darned dump except work," grumbled Sam in the safety of the vegetable garden, leaving Badge to haul the water.

"Aw, Sam! Dad's let us off each af'noon and you on'y sit around," protested Badge.

"What else is there to do? No pictures to go to, not even a newsreel. Nowhere to buy a lolly or an ice-cream or a bottle of pop. No hits to listen to on the radio and not even a dashed football to kick around. Why, even at home there's rabbits to trap. I made sixteen shillings last hols with the skins, and selling the rest to Mum. Come 'way out in the bush and your Dad don't own a trap and says there's no rabbits! Gor!"

"Dad snares a 'roo sometimes for dinner, but not in our valley. There's nothing here to trap without it's some liddle critture like Ticcy. You wouldn't want his fur, would you?"

"Why not? If it sells. You're soft, that's what you are."

With an effort, Badge went on watering though his hand was not quite steady. He tried to cool down by telling himself Sam was like a perky bird that flies in through the window thinking it sees crumbs; it finds there aren't any—being too flustered to see them there; it dashes itself round (and anyone that tries to help it) till it gets out again. You had to go gentle: you didn't have to fight a bird like that, or it never saw the crumbs.

"It's good-oh taking the sledge out," he said at last. "We can sit on—when we don't bump off!"

"Let's go and get the horse, then. I've done enough watering," said Sam, who had done none at all.

The sledge was the usual fork of a tree with upright spars driven in to hold the lengths of timber in place. Even Sam admitted it took brains and balance to remain on when the point rammed itself into a snag. They had magnificent fun behind placid old Prince, seeing who could cling on longest, and arrived at the paddock in bellows of laughter.

Dad was watching with a smile crinkling the corners of his eyes. "I cut a stack ready for you," he said. "You can load up on your own without me. I'm going to take a look round and see what the weather's up to—I reckon we're in for another spell o' dry."

He picked up his axe and disappeared into the bush to the south. Badge knew he often went "to look at the weather," and whatever he said, when he returned, whether wet or dry, Dad would not be far wrong.

"You bet we can load up as good as Uncle Dave," Sam told Badge, and astonished him by keeping at it, without a rest, till the end.

"Watch the speed finals. Giddup, there, old Dobbin!" he shouted, in high spirits because he was pleased with himself, and charged off down the hill with the load.

Of course he was going too fast and they struck a snag and the whole thing overturned, but after a hasty glance round to find out if Dad had seen, they put it right, and loaded afresh between new gusts of laughter.

Oh, it was grand to have a cobber like Sam!

They came round the last bend in style. Badge hoped Bron and Sheppie might be watching from the veranda, but he didn't expect Prince to pull up short and to find Bron just in front, waving her apron.

"Get away, you silly coot!" shouted Sam, the scowl coming back on his face.

"Aw, Bron, any horse but Prince would have shied at you! What's the matter?" Badge gasped.

"Nothing's the matter. She's just mad," Sam snarled.

"I was coming to fetch you!" Bron gulped, looking frightened. "He sent me. Somefin's happened."

69

"Nearly got yourself run over," Sam shouted. "What's happened and who sent you?"

"Uncle Dave did!" shrieked Bron as she turned and fled.

The boys exchanged a look and allowed Prince to plod forward soberly. They hitched him to the fence and hurried up the slope to the house.

Liddle-ma was on the veranda, smiling. "Come on, you two!" she called. "We're going away."

"Who's going away?"

"We are. All of us."

"Us too? And Bron and Sheppie?" Badge had to get it clear: such an unbelievable thing had never happened before.

"Ah," said Sam to Badge, "good, we're going home." But he didn't look altogether pleased.

"An' Ticcy?" asked Sheppie, hopping round Liddle-ma like a mosquito. "Take Ticcy, too?"

Liddle-ma paused to think a minute, then she said, "Yes, we'll take Ticcy, too," and the door banged behind her.

12

Preparing for Adventure

D AD shouted they were to unload the sledge before
they went inside, and to take Prince back to the
stable.

"It don't make sense," Badge cried, shaking his head in
bewilderment.

"Ah," said Sam as they got to work, "I know what's
happened. Mum's well and Dad's come to fetch us home.
Mum, she'll be worrying I don't get enough to eat out
your place, Badge. Mum knows I don't like fried termarters," he added with a side glance at his cousin.

Badge shook his head. "If Uncle Link was here, he'd
by magging away to my Dad, wouldn't he? And why
would we all go to the Farm? And didn't Uncle Link say
he was going away to Hobart?"

Sam rode the empty sledge back to the stable while
Badge led the horse. They found Dad there, unrolling a
big tarpaulin, and Sam sprang off to run and question
him.

"No," said Dad, "he's not here. Why would your Dad
come before the moon's full? I reckon he's on'y too glad
of the peace and quiet with you all gone. You two boys

71

can help carry this up to the house when you've fed Prince, and I'll tell you what we plan to do."

Sam peeled the harness from Prince as quick as skinning an onion, while Badge crammed his rack with hay; and there they were, dancing helpfully round Dad, ears cocked for news.

"After I left you . . ." began Dad, taking his time and studying the great waterproof sheet spread on the ground, "I got on top a hill looking over the south, and I seen—— hey!" he broke off, "kick that lump o' mud off the edge, there! It'll weigh enough for poor ole Prince to carry without we take the earth, too."

"Yes, Uncle Dave? What did you see?" urged his nephew.

"Why's Prince got to carry this?" Badge wanted to know.

"I seen the weather'd took up," Dad answered absently. "Likely to be fine for the next few days, I reckon."

"Was that all? Auntie told us that," Sam looked his disgust. "But she said we were going away?"

"And I seen," Dad continued, unhurried, "I seen a liddle brindle cow, Sam, which was a calf Old Bow'ra throwed. One what got away and went bush. Seen her plain as I see you two boys, for all she was down at the bottom of a valley out there."

"Aw, Dad, I know! You're going to try and bring her in?"

"I'm a-going to try, son. We're all a-going to try and round up the little brindle and maybe drive her into Old Bow'ra's paddock. With luck we'll have a new Bow'ra in milk next summer."

"But it's now you want the milk and butter," objected

72

Sam, "and, look, if girls come . . . well, you know what Bron's like, Uncle Dave! Jumps at the shadow of a leaf. And if we take a baby out with us——!"

Dad scratched his chin and his eyes twinkled as they rested on Sam. "So you're all set to come too, are you, son?"

"Course I am!" Sam scowled and flushed and looked at his boots.

"We may camp a night, we may camp a week or more in country I never rightly cut me way through, Sam. Can't leave anyone home not knowing where we are nor what's happened; can't take you back to the Farm first, seeing your Dad's in Hobart, can I? What's more I need every man jack o' you—and the horses, too—if we're to have a hope o' turning that cow. So you're welcome to come, son, on'y pull your belt in a couple o' holes and be glad if you get anything as good as fried termarters to fill your belly."

"And Narrups? Will we take him, too?" Badge asked eagerly.

"He's for the nippers to ride: feed him well tonight. I'll see to Prince and Di'mond, they got to carry all our gear. This," Dad stooped to straighten a wrinkle, "we got to take home to fix up with ropes tonight for it's all the shelter we'll have—without we strike a handy cave out there."

"Out where, Dad? To the south, like?" Badge asked, turning to stare at the far blue ranges of no man's land. "Will we get close up to that hill you showed with the rocks all broke on top like teeth—where the devils was—Devils' Hill?"

"We'll get where the brindle cow leads us, son, and that's any place short of the sea. Stop nattering now and

get this thing folded. You and Sam nip down the other end."

At home all was excitement and glorious confusion with bundles strewn all over the floor. The table was stacked high with loaves of soda bread cooling and filling the air with their rich, crusty smell. One loaf was still baking in the round, iron camp-oven with its flat lid, upon which Liddle-ma was piling the red, glowing embers.

The boys had dropped their load on the veranda and now sniffed round hungrily. "What's for tea, Bron?"

"*Good!*" She smacked her lips and stirred importantly at a large pot. "Spuds mashed with pork dripping and a few bits of meat in."

"And no pinching bits off them loaves!" called Liddle-ma sharply. "That's all we got to take with us, and who knows how long we'll be camping in the bush without bread?"

Ticcy was out, lapping his milk while Sheppie watched him. "Make Ticcy's housie?" she begged, clutching Badge by the sleeve.

"Leave him be, Sheppie!" Liddle-ma pushed hair back from her hot face. "Badge'll fix a box to carry Ticcy when he's had his tea, won't you, son? Bring your plates and sit on anything you can find round the fire—you can't use the table."

Badge was glad they didn't sit as usual on up-ended logs or benches before the newspaper cover on the old boards; he thought it a much more wonderful beginning to eat from their laps, their faces glowing and toasting in the heat as they shovelled the food down hungrily. And— *why* were they so hungry? Was it the excitement in the air that made them all ask Bron for a second helping?

Dad came in and had his, not sitting on a bundle of oddments, but on a corner of the table, with Liddle-ma. At the end, while he stirred his tea, he handed out jobs.

"Rub fat in your boots tonight and take spare socks. If the laces don't look too good I'll cut a spare strip o' leather for anyone as asks," were part of his instructions; but he also had special jobs allotted to each one, right down to Sheppie.

"You got to look after that young possum," said Dad. "And mind he don't walk off up a gum tree, for if he does that—well, Sheppie, *there he'll stop*."

"Sheppie have Ticcy?" requested that young lady, darting appealing looks from Badge to Dad and back to Badge again.

"No, Sheppie!" cried Bron in squeaky agitation. "You know he belongs to Badge. You may look after him, that's all."

"Want Ticcy!"

"Aw," said Badge, "if she wants him terribly, I'll give him to her."

"No!" said Liddle-ma. "See first how she looks after him out in the bush, Badge. If she brings him back all right, you can think about giving him to her then, son."

"One thing—and I reckon it's the most important if we don't want to have the place burned down, and start a bush fire into the bargain whiles we're miles away—who's to fetch water from the crik to douse the fire?"

"I could?" Bron suggested, looking inquiringly at Liddle-ma, while Sam frowned at the great hot bed of ashes, nearly a foot thick.

"No, Bron, seeing you got to get Sheppie and Ticcy and your own things over to Narrups for loading up. Nor Badge, seeing he's got to fetch the big horses for Dad and me to load. So . . . what about you, Sam?"

He did not sound exactly eager, but he said, "All right, Auntie."

"Pour it on till there's no spark left, then," said Dad, "and anyone late up tomorrer gets only cold tucker to eat.

Get going with what you all got to do tonight, and be out o' bed before there's a cheep out of the dawn." He stood up, stretched, and yawned. "I reckon Liddle-ma and me won't hit the fern till all hours," he sighed, "will we, mate?"

13

In Search of a Track

THE sun popped up between two rocky Fists and tinted pale pink a ripple of fleecy little clouds; black jays flew round uttering rude, raucous cries as if laughing or jeering at the little cavalcade about to set forth into the unknown.

"All set?" called Dad from the top of the line. He had swung Sheppie to her place in front of Bron, on the pony. She sat there beaming down at him, clutching the box which held Ticcy in front of her, while Bron clutched her tightly round the waist.

"I don't reckon this tarpaulin's too good"—Badge was adjusting Prince's load—"don't it need something more to balance the other side, Dad?"

"That's right, son." He walked round Prince, then looked up the slope towards home where Liddle-ma was hurrying down with the last load. "Nip up and fetch them things from her," he said. "We'll hang them on this side. Where's Sam?"

"Sam's coming," called Liddle-ma. "He's gone to fix the fire. It's the last thing to do, there's nothing more to fetch down, Dave, and I'll go back now and see everything's left safe and sound."

"Good, mate. It's time we was on the move. Did you close the shutters over the winders?"

"I did that. There's nothing but to see Sam's left the fire safe—*what's up?*" A sudden yell from Bron and a hollow-sounding crash made Liddle-ma break off and reach the pony in quick running strides. Ticcy's box was upside-down on the ground, with the little possum clinging to it dazed with fright, while Sheppie was fighting Bron's hold in order to slide down and rescue her pet.

"She let it out " gasped Bron. "I didn't see what she was up to . . . I grabbed the box an' it fell—we nearly felled off, too, all because she must let it out!"

"Why did you do that, Sheppie?" Liddle-ma asked as she restored order and stroked the panting little creature. "You might have hurt poor Ticcy bad."

Sheppie made no answer in words but doffed her red beret and offered it to her aunt like a collection bag in church.

"Oh?" Liddle-ma smiled as she popped Ticcy in it. "You want to hold him a minute to say 'sorry,' do you?"

But Sheppie held the red bag only long enough to make sure he was snug inside before tucking beret and all within the front of her coat. Then she grinned over her shoulder at Bron, and darted a glance of triumph through her hair at Liddle-ma.

The coat was an old one of Iggy's given to Sheppie to wear for the expedition, and it certainly was roomy. So when Bron started to scold, Liddle-ma said, "Let her be; if she can keep Ticcy safe there till the day hots up and she wants to take off her coat, why, she's welcome. I'll fasten the box on one of the pack saddles."

"I'll take it," Dad said. "You start Narrups going, mate,

and the rest of us'll catch up. We'll be here a month o' Sundays if we don't git a move on."

With Liddle-ma walking alongside, Narrups led the procession. Behind, with a fair gap, came Prince loaded like a Christmas tree, and Diamond—who was Sam's special charge—carrying the horses' own fodder. The boys trudged beside.

Lastly came Dad in his old bluey coat and battered, wide-brimmed hat, looking along the line to see the loads balanced properly. Sometimes he stared away to the south as though choosing a path, for the sun was higher now and had stretched out the hills.

"We'll give the horses a rest at the top o' the slope," said Dad after they had been going some time and had left Old Bow'ra's paddock quite a distance behind. "Pass the word along, son."

The known bush was ending with the skeleton track they were following. It turned east at the top of the slope and led to the big cattle run where the bullocks were, while their own direction lay somewhere to the unknown south.

Dad came to take his place at the head of the cavalcade, but first the horses were hitched in the shade while the walkers sank down to rest their weary legs.

"Do I light a fire for the billy?" asked Badge.

"No, son. A fire's too risky out here, in no time it'd get away and start a bush fire. We must do without tea," he sighed, "without we can make it in the dry bed of some crik."

"Ticcy's firsty," Sheppie announced, being very hot herself under the coat she had kept on for the little creature's sake, for the sun struck fiercely now from the clear blue sky.

"I reckon Ticcy's asleep," smiled Liddle-ma. "But bring your mugs along for water. I filled the billy full. Bron's got the bag with some lunch for each of us."

Bron doled out the packets with hunks of soda bread inside, spread with dripping or honey, and carefully collected back the wrappings afterwards, for paper was precious.

"I'll take a look round and get me bearings," Dad said as soon as he had finished. "You boys like to come?"

They sprang up, feeling important, and in a few steps the bush closed round them looking exactly the same in every direction—it seemed they could never, never find their way back again. But Dad marched forward through the scrub as though it was a highroad. "Somewheres about here," he said, "we can see out over that valley where I seen Brindle," and after they had scrambled over boulders and tree trunks and pushed their way through ferns and saplings, they topped a ridge—and there it was!

"Aw, Dad! We can't get down here?" Badge and Sam stared in dismay at a sheer drop of several hundred feet before them, while Dad's eyes quartered the valley like a hawk after a bandicoot, trying to see a clear space where a brindle cow might be grazing.

"That's right, son. We got to go right along and come down the top end o' the valley where there's no cliff, and cross there. Maybe she'll be up that end, Brindle, and maybe she'd be down here under our noses all the time."

"You were lucky to see her before, weren't you," Sam said, "with all that forest down there?"

"We got to see her, Sam—or else find her tracks. And we got to find a place up that end where we can camp for the night. So we best get going now, boys." As Dad turned and led the way back he added, "You're right,

Sam, the myrtle's thick enough down there in places, but I reckon it'll be worse trying to get off of this range into the valley. Rough and tough it'll be."

"But you've got a compass in your pocket, haven't you, Uncle Dave?" asked Sam with one half-frightened backward eye-sweep over the sameness of the unending bush. "You wouldn't come—you'd be lost without one, wouldn't you?"

His uncle only laughed. Badge explained proudly. "When Dad went prospecting for gold the other chaps used to call him 'the 'uman compass'—didn't they, Dad?"

"All the same, son, I were lost—well and truly bushed —that day I happened to look down from Three Fists when the mists lifted, and there, another step and I'd have landed in our valley—quicker nor a 'plat' sinks from sight, down I'd have come."

"There was a compass at Mrs. Jolly's, where I was in the city," Sam muttered. "I wish I'd brought it. Too right, I do!"

"What for, son? I bin tole there's minerals out these parts will give any compass the willies. If you can't trust your compass you're better without one, to my way o' thinking."

"There's Liddle-ma!" cried Badge in astonishment as they stepped suddenly in sight of the place where the horses were hitched. It seemed Dad's compass was in order.

On and on, the sun blazing overhead and the horses swishing their tails at a bevy of flies; on till the rocky ridge sloped to meet the forests of the valley and the sun was blotted out by green leaves. Still no sign, no track left by a straying cow.

"Keep a look-out for a place to camp, mate," Dad called back to Liddle-ma. "There's a big gully down here and maybe Brindle followed it down. I want to look round whiles there's still daylight. And remember, you nippers, I'll skin any one of you alive who puts his great foot down to spoil a hoof mark!"

On again, till the horses stopped before the trunk of an immense tree which had fallen on a bank, making a broad bridge. They could have walked beneath it, but Dad thought Brindle might have done this very thing, and halted them while he looked for her tracks.

The boys looked longingly at the roots sticking out where it had heeled over, inviting them to climb on top. They forgot they were tired. "I don't reckon the cow walked over that tree trunk?" Badge grinned, and Sam winked back knowingly as he scrambled to be first up: "No tracks up here!"

Liddle-ma, meanwhile, had lifted Sheppie down, and while she and Bron stretched their stiff legs was poking about in the dry space underneath. "This'll do for our camp, Dad!" she called, her voice sounding funny and hollow. "If you fix the tarpaulin at the back we'll be as snug as a bug in a rug under here."

In no time the camp was made. There were plenty of ferns for a springy mattress, but they dared not light a fire. Only cold food was handed round, and water from a billy. Then Dad hurried off to continue his search for tracks before daylight faded from the sky.

"Sheppie's asleep," said Liddle-ma presently. "You three can take a look round if you don't go far and get lost. I'm going to find a crik to fill the billy."

They watched her disappear through the trees; then Badge scrambled to his feet. "Come on, Sam," he said.

"You an' Bron and me might happen on a hoof mark what Dad missed."

"No, thanks," Sam yawned, "not if we got to take Bron with us I'm not coming. We'd never see a thing, she'd yell out about snakes or something all the time."

And Bron, who had been about to say she would stay with Sheppie, whined and called her brother a mean pig. "I'll go on my own and *I'll find a track before you do,* Sam!" she threatened bravely. But then, noticing how dark it was growing under the trees, she added hastily, "I don't mean tonight—it's too late to see tonight, isn't it, Badge?"

"That's right," said Badge to keep the peace, and sighed deeply.

14

Bron Keeps Her Word

THERE was no breath of wind in the forest, nothing to make the tarpaulin rustle, yet Badge could hear a little rustling sound near his ear.

He rolled over and pushed back a blanket, for the night was sultry. The insistent little sound went on. He sat up and looked at the others sleeping under the great bulge of the tree trunk: the sound came from the corner where Sheppie was curled against Liddle-ma and at once he saw what it was—Ticcy was moving behind the wire-netting of his box, chewing fresh gum leaves.

Badge reached out an arm and drew the box a little nearer, so that he could watch him. He did not feel at all sleepy. There were possums outside, too; he could hear a big "brush" calling to his mate with hoarse, coughing barks, and judged they were running down the tree trunk over his head. Far away an owl grieved mournfully.

Suddenly there was a brief, angry snarl and something thumped down only a few yards away and scratched at one of the bags. In an instant Dad's hand shot out and whatever it was vanished out into the night. Dad started to move the bags and Badge padded over to him.

85

"What was it, Dad?" he whispered.

"Tiger cat, son. After our meat. Don't reckon it'll come again now, but I'll move these things and sleep the other side."

When he had helped put the food in a safer place, Badge asked about cow tracks, for he had been asleep when Dad returned.

"Didn't see so much as the shadder o' the skerrick of a track from that darned cow. If she's not up this end we got to work right down into the thick bush, son, and by then who knows where she'll have got to? Best get some sleep, now. Termorrow you must all walk round with your eyes skinned."

"Good-oh, Dad." Cow tracks or no cow tracks, this was the life Badge loved, and he was deeply content. Slapping at the mosquitoes that pinged around he glanced at the gray hump which was Sam. As he snuggled down he smiled to himself, thinking Sam must be liking it, too; for look—only *once* all yesterday had he spoken of Mrs.-Jolly-where-I-was-in-the-city!

Bron ventured a little way along the thread of track worn by wombats and stopped, gazing round fearfully. Liddle-ma had promised that no snakes would be out of their holes at this chilly hour of dawn, but . . . well, there were other things, lots of other horrible, frightening things waiting to get you if you were alone.

"I reckon I can do without a wash," she whispered to herself, after going a little farther and losing the comfortable camp sounds in the distance. "She won't know if I rub me face with me hanky."

Yet she hesitated, longing to be brave enough to reach the small trickle of water described by Liddle-ma as "ten

hops of a 'roo along a track you can't miss"—yearning to
please this great strong person who had captured so much
of her starved little heart. Her thin fingers twisted the
corner of her sacking apron as she stood peering ahead;
then she remembered how Liddle-ma had made it for her

from a sugar bag and put flowers on the pocket and her name in bright wool.

So Bron went on. She disturbed some small birds on the ground, but they rose and clapped their wings at her cheerfully and broke the awful silence. Then she heard Dad's axe going "ker-umph! . . . ker-umph! . . . ker-umph!" in the distance, clearing the horses a track for when they moved on after breakfast.

A stony bed showed where a creek would usually be flowing. Bron unwound the towel from her neck and made her toilet where water oozed between two rocks. Glowing as much from her achievement as from the cold water, she dared to stand and look round before bolting back along the path she had come. Something—some gleam of brilliant color—caught her eye. What could it be?

Curiosity made her push through scrub and scramble over a few ferny boulders and so step into the most beautiful place she had ever seen. A pool scooped deep in solid rock still held water, and this reflected the blue of the sky and the gorgeous scarlet flowers of waratah on bushes surrounding the small glade. Maidenhair and other dainty ferns foamed like lace in all the rocky cracks.

Sure that no one had seen what she now saw, Bron moved down determined to pick Liddle-ma some of those flowers as big as her own fist. She had to work her way round some dense growth, but on the other side was a space of smooth rock. Pushing the fern fronds back she stepped out—only to stand rooted with fear at what lay, round and black, in the open space.

Fear of snakes had been bred in her from the day when she was not much older than Sheppie and had come on one coiled round and round, sleeping on a bank in the sun. True, it had lifted its head and, seeing her, had shaken out its coils in a breath and been gone . . . the horror remained.

Therefore, before anything else she let out a lusty, high-pitched scream. She did not try to get away, just stared with popping eyes and yelled. But the noise she made did not seem to disturb it in the least. After a time this struck her as strange and she stopped.

Dad, crashing through the bush, reached her at the same time as Sam and Badge who had followed the track, directed by Liddle-ma.

"Where's the snake? Where did it go?" Sam shouted, waving a stick.

"What snake, Sam? I wasn't yelling for an ole snake," Bron told him with dignity, "I thought Uncle Dave'd like to see I'd found the cow's track." She pointed to the round, black cow pat lying on the rock, showing where Brindle had passed and paused for a drink.

Dad put an arm round her shoulders and looked down at the plain, pointed little face. "Bron, *you beaut!*" he exclaimed.

Sam looked with curled lip at Dad crouched on the ground, noting every sign in the dust with happy excitement. "What a fuss about cow droppings! If Mrs. Jolly——"

"But Dad's finding out things," Badge interrupted quickly. "He's finding out how long since Brindle was here, see? Bron's found the track and now we got to foller it up."

"You two boys can nip back to breakfast," Dad called, lifting his head reluctantly a moment. "Tell Liddle-ma what's happened and say Bron and me'll be along in a tick."

"I knew it would never work," said Sam gloomily as they turned away, "bringing a girl out here. Now Bron'll be too big for her boots—you'll see!"

"Well, she said she'd find the cow track before you did, Sam, and she's done it, I reckon. Don't you?"

"You know nothing, Badge. You make me sick! There's some funny business somewhere; Bron only yells like that when she thinks she's seen a snake. And she wouldn't go off on her own in the bush, not for anything, so——*gosh!*" he broke off suddenly as they came in sight of the tree-trunk camp, *"ham for breakfast!"* and raced ahead.

Yes, it was the ham at last, and when Dad led Bron in like a princess with her great bunch of brilliant red flowers tied round with her towel, Liddle-ma handed her a wedge of ham cut like a slice of melon, and said, "Good on you, Bron! My word, we're all proud of you—aren't we, Sheppie?"

Everyone said, *"My word!"* and "Good on yer, Bron!" and Sheppie produced Ticcy for her to hold a minute as a supreme treat—till poor Bron, overwhelmed by so much happiness, dripped tears of joy on his fur, and Sheppie hastily snatched him back again.

It was a happy breakfast.

All day they followed signs and tracks, Dad going in front and stopping now and then to look, or notch a tree with his axe to blaze a path for coming home. The unseen cow led them across the valley and up the slopes of a range the other side. Here, in the full heat of the day, they stopped to eat and sleep a little, in the shade of the dainty, weeping foliage of a group of native cherry trees.

"There's not a skerrick of grass up here," said Liddlema as they prepared to move on again, looking at the weather-worn rocks ahead. "Why can't Brindle stay down in the valley where there's feed?"

"Could be she knows a better valley over there?" suggested Badge.

"That's right, son," Dad said as he clambered ahead of the horses. "Maybe she found the crik drying up back there with this long spell o' dry, maybe she knows of a river."

So they plodded on, tired but hopeful. Near the top they came to a wild, rough part where they lost the tracks completely—but picked them up again by chance in a narrow gully. Once through this they were over the range, the ground sloping steeply towards a tangle of forest.

"Getting too dark to see the tracks," Dad said, calling a halt. "We'll climb on top there for a look-out, when we've hitched the horses."

Dad's look-out was a jutting spur with a flat top: it was not hard to climb. As Badge hauled himself over and stood upright he gave a gasp, "Look, Dad!—the Devils' Hill!" and pointed to great crags like a fortress topping a hill on the other side of the curving valley.

Dad nodded briefly: his eyes were on the valley itself; it ran roughly east and west. Deep down was the sheen of water flashing here and there. "Can't see her in this light, o' course," said Dad, "but it's a good valley . . . open . . . I reckon a fire's cleaned it out not many years back. Ought to spot Brindle in the daytime."

"Aw, Dad, it's . . ." Words failed Badge as he gazed

91

with all his eyes at the wild beauty of mountain and forest. A blaze of color from the setting sun streamed from the west, turning the depths to gold and Devils' Hill to a rich, fiery red.

"That hill's like carrots when you scrape 'em," said Bron, "and down there . . ." she paused, having no words for the royal gilding that dressed the depths with such splendor.

"Down there," said Sam, peering carefully at Devils' Hill, "down near the bottom there's a crack like a cave, all black, which runs right up."

"Leave your sunset valley now," said Liddle-ma, unknowingly giving it a name for all of them, "we got to find a place to camp the night."

15

The Cavern

DAD found some fairly level ground and they camped where they were, on the heights. He was afraid if they went down into Sunset Valley they would lose or trample over Brindle's trail.

"I want a possum to shin up this tree with a rope," he said standing before a stunted gum. A burst of laughter greeted Sheppie's kind offer to let Ticcy try. "I was meaning more a monkey," Dad explained. "We'll see how Sam gets on, will we, Sheppie?"

Sam climbed well and soon had the rope slung like a washing line; over this they threw the tarpaulin for a tent. The ground was too hard to guy it out with pegs but there were plenty of boulders to use as weights once the sides were stretched out.

"We won't sleep too soft tonight," Liddle-ma sáid as she looked in vain for ferns or springy scrub, "and we'll have to go careful on the water in the billies, too."

"But we can have a great, big roarin' camp fire and a mug o' tea at last!" Dad rejoiced. "You boys nip round and fetch in all the dry stuff you can lay hands on before it's dark. No fear o' starting a bush fire on them bare rocks."

He moved downhill himself to prize up a weathered stump he had noticed in a little hollow. Badge heard him jump suddenly and swear. He called, "What's up, Dad?" —for Dad always said he "didn't hold with cursin' and swearin', for what was the sense of it?"

"Come and see—quick!"

As he jumped over a rock Badge called Sam and the two ran down. Dad was standing with his weight on one leg with something shimmering and threshing about round his boot.

"Snake," Dad informed them without moving. "Hole under the stump, and he didn't go much on being roust out. Near got me finger—no time to pick up a stick so I trod on where he keeps his brains. I reckon he's dead now, but a snake'll always go on wriggling till the sun's down— did you know that, son?"

Sam nodded. "That's what Dad says."

"Hadn't I best give him a bash or two, before you takes your foot off of him?" asked Badge.

"No. He's a thick chap, no call to spoil the skin, it'd make a fine belt." Dad stepped aside as he spoke.

Neither Badge nor Sam could help a feeling of revulsion and horror as they stared at the thick coils jerking as though alive; but the spasms grew less and soon the snake lay still. "Ah!" said Dad simply, with a jerk of his thumb to the west. The sun had gone, leaving only fiery clouds behind as it dipped from sight.

"Could I have him?" Sam asked, as Badge was gingerly lifting the snake at the end of a long stick.

"You can have him, Sam—though you got that fine belt your Mum gave you, haven't you? But don't waste all night skinning it. There's plenty firewood to be got."

94

He walked away. Badge let the snake slither to the ground and Sam came and prodded it with his toe. "She's a beaut! Look, Badge, I don't want it. Not for a belt for me, I mean. This one Mum got me cost quids." He fingered its many gadgets lovingly, smiled at his cousin and slowly winked, "But I got an idea. It's for Bron I want the snake—see?"

"Good on you, Sam!" Badge beamed at him happily. "My word, it's an idea—she'll reckon you're Christmas! That old red thing she wears is no more good than rotten wood." He opened his sharp knife and dropped to his knees for the skinning.

"Hey—stop! What you doing?" gasped Sam. "I didn't mean you to *skin* it! I didn't mean that!"

"Want to do it yourself? All right?"

"Well . . . I meant . . ."

"Us to do it together, eh? Good-oh!"

"Yeah." Sam sighed, defeated by Badge's stupidity, pulled out his knife, and came close. "But look, we won't tell Bron it's for her—not yet."

"No, thass right. Any road it won't be ready till after we gets home and pegs it out."

Badge worked quickly to be done before dark. Sam held the skin and helped but he seemed oddly bewildered—almost as though he found himself doing something he hadn't intended at all.

They had mashed potatoes with ham for tea and went to bed soon after: the night was cold and the fire lacked wood, but at least Dad got his billy tea. "What's up, mate?" he called. "What you fussing over?"

Liddle-ma stuck her head out from the tent. "I can't find the other bag o' flour, Dave, and we're nearly through the bread. I wanted to be all set for making damper for breakfast."

"Leave it be till morning. It'll turn up in daylight," Dad answered easily.

But it didn't. It couldn't be found anywhere.

"It was on Prince when we set out, for I seed it," Badge told them. "Must've come unhitched and dropped off and we never noticed?"

"We still got the little bag. Best hurry on and find that cow, then we'll turn for home and won't need much more tucker." Dad looked worried all the same.

Brindle's tracks went round the myrtle forest and were clear to see; they led down into Sunset Valley. Before the worst heat of the day broke on them they were through dense scrub and out on level ground. At once the horses' heads went down to graze the sweet, wiry grass.

"We're there!" Dad called happily.

They were there. The cliffs where they had stood at sunset looked tremendous seen from below, and Devils' Hill on the other side a great, rocky tower with battlements on top. Between the two lay the deep valley. It curved like Dad's grass-cutting sickle where the Hill bulged into it on the southern side, narrowed to the west, and was hot as an oven.

From where they halted on the eastern slopes they could look partly down, for—as Dad had noticed—a fire had swept through in recent years. They could see pools of water and the extraordinary green of the place, could smell the scent of unseen flowers and hear the clamor of honey-eating birds.

"Aw, Dad—it's not like this out home?" Badge stared, awed, at scarlet flowers against rich greens. A flock of parrots no less brilliant was cleaving the humid air.

Dad allowed himself a minute to look round while he mopped his face. "Too right, son—or we'd never get no work done," he panted. "I reckon this place stays warm all winter—them rocks holds the heat in—and holds the wet, too. Look over there," he pointed to Devils' Hill, which had a silvery line gleaming like a snail's track from a cleft near the top, right down its face; "that spills over in winter so we can see it way out on top o' Three Fists. I pointed it out, one time, to Badge."

"Meaning it comes down like a waterfall, Unk?" Sam asked, quite impressed. "But why would water come out of that crack?"

"Maybe there's a holler on top and a bit o' a tarn, Sam, and it seeps through, like. Now"—his eyes were back on the green grass again "—we'll hobble Narrups and let the horses graze. Find yourselves a shady spot for a bit o' shut-eye, but watch out for snakes. Later we'll look around for a place to camp. I'm going now to have a look-see down the valley for that cow."

"Won't you have a bit o' tucker first?"

"Give me a bit in me pocket, mate. I want to come on her before she knows we're here." He slung a coil of rope from his shoulder and instructed Badge to ride down with another if he called.

"Aw. Dad—how d'you know she's in this valley?"

Dad pointed out some dried cakes of cow dung in the grass. "I reckon this is Brindle's home," he smiled, his eyes gleaming with contentment. "She came away, maybe, on'y to ask a gen'leman friend in the cattle run to break out an' share it with her."

"But the boy friend said, 'T'aint worth the trouble'?"

"That's it, son."

"Poor Brindle, she must be lonely," Bron suggested.

97

"She'll like being back in our paddock. We'll talk to her."

After Dad vanished down the valley they had a meal, eating the last of the ham to the bone, and tried to rest. It seemed Sunset Valley teemed with insect life as well as birds and flowers; leeches and mosquitoes troubled them, and a six-foot black snake slithered from sight when Liddle-ma dipped water from a pool that was as lovely as fairyland. She didn't mention this but gave each one of the older children instructions to cut a strong, whippy stick, to carry always "just in case."

Sam seemed excited and restless. "Can I go on down there and have a look at the hole I saw in Devils' Hill? We could camp there, Auntie, away from the 'squitoes."

" 'Squitoes can fly, son, and how would we get the junk up there—even supposing you boys climbed in?"

"Leeches don't fly or climb, Liddle-ma. Can I go along with Sam?"

"Don't they? This big one's just climbed up me. Or flown here!"

"*Ow!*" screamed Bron, springing from the ground. "Somefing's in there! It—it wriggled!"

The wriggler proved to be a harmless lizard, nothing worse, but Liddle-ma decided the shady spot gave no rest to any but Sheppie—who was awake now, happily searching for "iccle wigglers to play wiv Ticcy."

So she hooked the packs back on the horses, swung the two girls on the pony and led the way to the middle of Sunset Valley, where the rocky foot of Devils' Hill was gashed by a black hole about twenty feet up.

"Good-oh! We can get in—those fallen blocks are like

98

steps," Sam gloated. "We'll get the junk up easy—won't we, Badge?"

All they could see from below was a black slit and the rocky staircase, up which the boys climbed like monkeys. Liddle-ma hitched the horses and waited, not taking Sam's idea seriously but wanting him to see for himself how useless it would be for a camp.

A head bobbed from behind a great squarish mass and Badge's face beamed down on her. "Look!" he cried, reaching out his hand and cupping it against a shiny patch of the wall. He held it there a minute and water dripped from his fingers as he brought it to his mouth and drank.

"Oo!" Bron waved to him excitedly. "See, Badge has got water up there like from a tap!"

Higher than Badge, Sam was leaning over and calling eagerly, "Come on up—it's easy! There's a hugeous, beaut great cavern up here for us to live in. Come on up and see, Auntie!" Then he coaxed, "Everything laid on! Water? —yes! And a fair bit of firewood from a tree that's crashed over. And just wait till you see inside!"

16

"Snip Go the Shears"

SOME hours later, near sunset, Dad came back from the western end of the valley with no cow. He stopped in amazement on seeing puffballs of smoke coming from a hole in Devils' Hill.

A head popped over the lip. "Hey, Dad!" yelled Badge, "this is our new camp. Sam found it and it's a beaut!"

Other heads bobbed up and black hands waved to Dad against a background of smoke. "Well, strike me pink," he laughed, "a home in Devils' Hill. And, bejabers, a row o' little black devils live in it—if that don't beat all!"

"Did you see Brindle?" squeaked Bron.

Dad shook his head. He made a great pretense of being afraid to venture into the cavern, and of not being able to climb up there in any case, when invited in.

"Come on, Unk—I'll help you." Sam quickly scrambled down. "It's easy if you follow me."

He led his docile uncle from rock to rock till they stood in the wide mouth of the cave. The floor had been neatly swept with brooms of gum leaves, and a fireplace cunningly made of blocks of stone. Some smoke swirled inside, but most of it blew out into the valley. The stones held an assortment of billies and pots over hot embers.

"Good!" said Dad, pausing to sniff with satisfaction.

Liddle-ma removed a lid and stirred. "Pea soup. The end of the ham bone. You ready?" she asked.

"No, no!" Sam protested. "This is the dining-room, we got to show him the bedroom end yet."

"Be quick then, or it'll burn."

They rushed Dad across the floor of stone. The cavern did not go back very far: it narrowed and the roof sloped down till it met great blocks and columns of stone. The fading light showed cracks and holes where there were dry bones. The place reeked of some wild animal.

Bron tugged gently at his coat and looked back at the firelight for courage. Sam wrinkled his nose and said, "That's the end. Pooh, what a stink! We don't need to come back here, though. Look!"

Dad looked and saw the tarpaulin neatly spread in a place sheltered and walled off by the natural stone. Sheppie, clutching Ticcy in her arms, kindly jumped about on top to show Dad how springy a bed it would be, because of the soft green ferns they had stuffed underneath.

"My word! I'll say this for you—you kids have worked,"

Dad praised them. "How did you get the junk up?—this, fer instance?" His eyes moved from the tarpaulin to the pile of blankets on it.

"Easy!" boasted Sam. "We got a rope—the one you left with Badge. And we got the stuff on Prince, and made him stand just below . . ."

He was stopped by a burst of laughter and went rather red.

"What's the joke?" Dad wanted to know.

"Nothing . . . only . . ." Suddenly Sam himself laughed and explained, "Well, see, Unk, I was the one passing the stuff up. I was standing on Prince (like I've seen at the circus) when he—well, he walked away!"

"And we yanked Sam up instead o' blankets, Dad," Badge told him. "You was the first junk to come up, wasn't you, Sam?"

"Might've broke his neck," they heard Liddle-ma comment. "Come and take a look at the valley. Then it's tea."

Look-Out Heights and all the other side were painted an amazing shade of red, while the valley itself was a river of smoky gold.

"Gosh! We did right to call it Sunset Valley," said Sam.

"H'mn," Dad scratched his chin. "But maybe if we'd named it Brindle Valley that flaming cow would have shown up."

The flaming cow who seemed invisible yet left her tracks in every clearing, nearly spoilt the evening for Dad. "See, mate, we got to find her soon or something'll happen."

"Like what, Uncle Dave?"

"Like running out o' tucker, now we lost that flour. Plenty o' 'roo back where I been today but no time to go snaring. And the bush as dry as a match, Sam. If a fire starts up, where'd we be?"

"Safe up here, snug in our cave."

Badge fixed wondering eyes on his father. "Aw, Dad! You said bush fires don't start theirselves, you said chaps knocked out a pipe or left a fire going, you said——"

"Yeah!" Sam backed him up. "We're the only chaps in this part of the world, Unk, and we don't light fires, do we?" He drew nearer to the blazing logs, for the cavern was cold now the sun was down. "Only in safe places like this, I mean."

"I hope, son, you doused the fire well before we left home? I meant to go back," Liddle-ma said, looking thoughtfully at Sam.

He scorned to answer such a childish question and demanded of Dad, "What else could happen out here, Unk? Would the devils get us?" and laughed loudly.

"The weather devils might, Sam. Nice job getting that flaming cow if it sets in wet. Smells to me a bit like a change coming." He got up and walked to the mouth of the cavern, his back to the bright light of the fire.

"*Look!*" he called, and something in his tone brought them running. There were no stars above and no valley below, nothing to be seen but gray mist.

Liddle-ma's voice said comfortingly, "I reckon with the water down there, after a hot day there's always fog. It's a queer, deep sort o' valley."

"Ough, it's cold!" Bron shuddered and went back to Sheppie, who had stayed to feed Ticcy and play with him.

"Yeah, but we got a good, snug home with a roof over our heads, Bron. You ought to be thankful," said Sam, without actually stating the person he felt should now be

103

thanked—only glancing hopefully for a sign of Dad's approval.

Dad gave him none. He remained lost, staring at the great wall of gray as though reading a book.

The mist was still there in the morning, and whatever Dad thought about it, the children secretly rejoiced. The gray fog was drawn across the cavern's entrance like a curtain over a window, closing them into a small world of their own; it made everything seem strange and different and slightly unreal, like opening your eyes under water.

They were tired and it was wonderful to lie long in bed. Sam was astonished to find he need not even pretend to be asleep; through half-closed eyes he saw Liddle-ma smiling at him as she stirred the porridge. "No call to get up unless you're hungry," she twinkled. "Dad's out doing the horses and he don't want you boys for he reckons you'll lose yourselves out there in this."

Finding they need not get up, they all became minded for breakfast. It was fun squatting round the fire stirring honey into a porridge bowl, knowing they might go back to their blankets afterwards if they liked.

Somehow no one did actually like; Bron and Sheppie because they had to feed Ticcy, the boys because they had to fetch him some fresh gum leaves—or so they told each other, though perhaps they both had other things more interesting to do than sleep, when it came to the point.

By afternoon, however, when they were still imprisoned in cloud, Sam grew restless.

"Gee, I wish I had a pack o' cards!"

"You couldn't play now. I'm going to shear the sheep."

Liddle-ma seated Sheppie on a convenient stone with a grayish towel round her and produced a pair of scissors. "I think Big Dog Sheppie wants to see out o' his eyes more?" she suggested, and—strangely—Big Dog Sheppie made no fuss at all.

Badge was used to the performance: his head had the usual jagged, saw-toothed effect when she finished with him, but Bron's came out neat and shiny, she having blissfully allowed her aunt to crop all she wanted of the straggling locks.

"You all look as fine as a blue wren with new feathers, except . . ." Liddle-ma paused and looked at Sam. He was kicking logs into the fire in a bored sort of way.

"Sam?" Bron finished for her, in the kind of whisper which makes everyone look up and prick their ears. "Oo, *no!* Mum, she'd have kittens if he lost his curls!"

Liddle-ma sent her to fetch a billy that was left outside, shook the towel and started to fold it up.

"Hey, what about me?" Sam demanded, once Bron was gone, and he perched himself on the barber's chair. "I got more on top to keep me warm than Badge had, Auntie."

"Thass right, son. Do I take it all off?"

"Yeah, all the sissy curls. Aw, here's Unk, wanting his turn."

"I'll take me turn in the line," said Dad as he climbed into the cavern.

Liddle-ma made her usual remark. "I charge for this; I belong to a union"; and Dad bellowed as he always did on hair-cutting days at home:

" 'Snip go the shears, boys—snip—snip—snip!' "

"But, Unk!" Sam objected. "Dad got that song from a shearing shed and *he* sings it: 'Clip go the shears . . .' "

"And my gran'father, he got it from England," said Liddle-ma, "and he sang: 'Ring the bell, watchman, ring—ring—ring!' "

"Aw, Dad, will you sing us 'Johnny Cakes'?" Badge begged, and Dad said maybe he would, maybe they'd have a bit of a sing-song round the fire after tea.

"We'll need a good fire," he added, "to warm our heads after all the wool's been taken off of 'em."

"Good-oh, Dad, we'll pile it on!"

It was a fine sing-song, and they only had to look at Sam to start a laugh, he looked so odd without his curls. Cutting them off seemed to have altered him—or perhaps this was a Sam they had never happened to meet before. He it was who suggested the new games, asked riddles, taught the latest hits, and made bed-time come long before they were ready.

"We can't go till Unk's sung 'Johnny Cakes' again!" protested Sam at the end. Dad groaned and started off again:

"With me little white flour bag a-sitting on the
  stump,

106

Me little tea and sugar bag looking nice and
    plump,
A little fat cod fish just off the hook,
And four little johnny cakes, a credit to the
    cook!"

"Stop!" cried Liddle-ma suddenly. "Did you hear that?"
"Hear what?"
"I thought . . . but it couldn't be . . ."
Breathless listening brought no sound to their ears
other than the hiss and rumble of the fire; gray mist still
muffled the valley, and Dad said it was, my word it was
—*bedtime!*
They were just snuggling down to sleep when it came
once more for all to hear, a ghostly, far-off, moaning cry.
Dad was pulling on his coat again and struggling into his
boots before it died away—for there was no doubt what
it was, that eerie bellowing.
"*Brindle!*" cried Badge and Liddle-ma, both at the same
instant.

17

Left in Charge

BADGE was sure he spent the whole night listening for another ghostly bellow, or Dad's return with news of Brindle. Actually, Dad came back from an unsuccessful hunt, slept a few hours and went out again, before his son was awake.

"Hey, Sam!" Reaching over, he prodded the gray cocoon near by till it humped itself and Sam's head appeared—a smooth head like a crestless cockatoo's. "Wake up, the mist's gone!"

Some pinky clouds were swimming languidly in the blue of the cavern's mouth, pushed along by a light breeze. The fire was low and there was no sign of either Dad or Liddle-ma.

Sam stared at their great window as though unable to believe what Badge had said, grinned to himself, and began to dress without a word. By signs, he told Badge not to disturb the sleeping Bron and Sheppie.

They stole away and climbed from the cavern into the miracle of sunshine; it stretched long arms and chased the shadows from the valley, warmed the rocks, broke into jewels the little beads of moisture left by mist and made them sparkle gloriously. Old Sun himself was back again and two boys welcomed him like a dear friend long given up for dead.

"Will we look for tracks?" Badge suggested.

"Or a cow? Gee!" Sam mentioned gloatingly, "Bron'll be mad as a snake when she wakes up and finds us gone."

Badge was listening intently. "Can't see no cow, can't hear no cow, but . . . there's something on the move . . . over the other side . . . by the long pool."

"Not a sound!" whispered Sam. "We'll stalk it."

He took the lead, creeping forward with great caution so as not to crackle a twirl of bark or roll a stone. At long last they approached the water's edge on their knees, gently pushing ferns and scrub aside with their hands, till Sam judged the time had come to stand and look. "She's in there!" he whispered right in Badge's ear, his eyes sparkling with excitement—"*Now!*"—and stood up.

"Hullo, son!" said Liddle-ma, lifting her head from the billies she was filling. "I reckoned it was you two boys I heard. Out looking for cow tracks?"

"That's right, Auntie. Did Unk see Brindle last night?"

"No, son. The mist was thick like a curtain till close on daybreak and since then we seen nothing."

"We all heard her holler out, didn't we, Liddle-ma?" Badge wanted to be reassured it had not all been a dream.

"We did, son, and Dad reckons she's on top there and the mist made the sound seem right in the cave. He's coming now, so he'll tell you. I'll go and rouse up some breakfast. Is Bron up?"

"Sleeping tight when we left."

"Did you think to put a bit o' wood on the fire?"

Dad didn't ask awkward questions, he told his plans at once. "No doubt of it, the flaming cow's on top o' Devils'

Hill, and I can't find how she gets up there." He seemed to speak his thoughts aloud as he stared at the rocky summit. "Might work her way up from the back—but it's steep there, too. If we cuts a track . . . ? No . . . a rock sent rolling'd startle the ole girl into a gallop ending at the South Pole. You any good at tracking a cow quietly, Sam?"

"Me? Oh, yeah, I been tracking lots of flaming cows with Dad, Unk."

"Did they hear you coming?"

Sam paused a moment, remembering the stalking of Liddle-ma, and avoided this delicate question with skill. "I can throw a rope, too, Unk. If we find her I might lasso her for you. Can Badge and me come, too?"

"I wouldn't mind taking one of you to help Liddle-ma and me round her up, but the other'd have to stay in the camp and look after the nippers."

Two pairs of eyes bored into Dad as he stood in the sunshine by the pool, scratching his chin thoughtfully. At last he said, "If I do take one o' you boys it'll have to be——" he looked across at the smoke rising cheerfully from the mouth of the cave. "Breakfast!" he announced abruptly.

"Which? Which one of us?" they demanded urgently. "You haven't said!"

"It'd have to be you, Sam."

"Good-oh, Unk!" Sam grinned his astonishment and relief. "I've seen no end of cows lassoed on the pictures. I'll show you."

"Aw—Dad!" protested Badge, in woeful disappointment.

"But best if you both stops behind, maybe," Dad concluded.

Sam wasn't going to be cheated like this; he brought

all his persuasion to work, and as Dad turned away he begged, "You can't leave me out of it now, Unk! You said you wouldn't mind taking one of us, and you said I'd be the one to go!"

"I did so, Sam—but now I'm going to tell Badge for why. See, son, Sam's not yet man enough for us to leave in charge of a camp with his two kid sisters, like I can leave you. That's why I'm taking him with me." And Dad turned his steps towards breakfast.

Sam watched him out of earshot and muttered, "Thanks! Well, soots me, old cock! All right, I'm not man enough to mind the kids, then! I'm better at catching cows than being a nursemaid—I know that," and he forced a laugh. But he did not look round at Badge and his face was rather red.

Under his usual shield of silence, Badge hid a heart choking with envy as he watched them depart without him. Somehow it made it worse that Sam did not forget to turn and wave, and carried the spare rope slung round his shoulders with such an air.

Dad's words were no comfort now—they were a mockery.

Tidying up and peeling spuds, helping Bron wash dishes and finding Sheppie's missing hair ribbon—were these jobs more "manly," he asked himself bitterly, than climbing an unknown height to capture a cow that was half wild?

"Badge?" Bron fixed on him small eyes gone misty with homage, adoring this wonderful, gentle cousin who had saved her from being left with Sam. "What'll we do now, Badge?"

That was just it—what was there to do?

111

"Have you fed Ticcy?"

"Oo, yes! Sheppie's only playing with him, pertending he's a dog and she's taking him for a walk."

The eyes fastened again, mutely saying of course he'd know something new and exciting for them to do—*of course!*

Down by the pool? But Liddle-ma had said not to take them in the valley. There was nothing new to do in the cavern, they'd done it all yesterday. If only Sam were here, he'd think of something in the wink of an eye. What was that game, now, that he got even Dad playing?

"What about a game o' guessing, Bron? 'I spy with my little eye something beginning with . . . with T.'"

Bron turned it down swiftly. "Sheppie, she was asleep when we played that. She's too little."

"Aw . . ." Oh, why wasn't Sam here!

Suddenly Sheppie bleated from the end of the cave, "Want Ticcy! Badge, *want Ticcy!*"

"She hasn't reely lost him, she just pertends."

But Sheppie called again, and though Bron said kindly,

"I'll go and see, Badge. You go on thinking what we're going to do," he was glad to hurry after her.

It was dark in the far, smelly end, where usually they never went. Ticcy was not to be seen on the ledges, nor the big lumps of stone which seemed to have split off the walls. He could not see Sheppie, either, and Bron suddenly screamed, "She's gone! Where are you, Sheppie? Sheppie's gone!"

"Want Ticcy!" The muffled voice came from behind what appeared to be a solid wall of stone.

Was this looking after her? Badge felt his heart pound as he climbed about seeking for her in the dim light, while Bron recited in a shrill voice all the awful things which could happen to a small child.

Sheppie herself was not much help, her mind was fixed on grabbing the exploring possum. It was not until they heard a triumphant "Got 'im!" that she stuck a hand up between two columns and showed them how to reach her.

"Oo! It's a big sort of hole—a tunnel—down here, and we never knew!" Bron exclaimed as she helped haul her sister out. She had to be lifted bodily, since both arms were wrapped round Ticcy. He seemed rather chastened and when they put him back in his box, went straight to bed.

Sheppie was not in the least chastened. When Bron began to worry again about what to do, she simply tugged Badge's belt and pointed to the far end.

"Want to go back in that hole, Sheppie?"

She looked at him and smiled, and the look was just as compelling without a veil of hair over her eyes, as when she peeped through a fringe.

"Oo, Badge—let's!" Bron agreed. "It looked like a big

tunnel—that's what it is. Sam doesn't know about it, does he? Let's us go see it, Badge?"

He took down Dad's special treasure, the big hurricane lamp. The problem of what to do was answering itself. "Get us a match, Bron."

"Come on, Sheppie—he's taking us! You are taking us, aren't you, Badge? Will we go for a long explore?"

As he turned the wick higher, he glanced at Bron, bobbing about with excitement. What had happened to the old, timid, scared-possum Bron? He did not realize it was only her faith in him which was making her so brave.

18

Sheppie's Astonishing Find

A GIRAFFE could have walked in that tunnel with its neck full stretch and never grazed its ears. It was choked with stones and rubbish except in the center of the narrow path, which Badge thought wild creatures kept smooth with the padding of their paws. He stopped and raised the lamp high to look ahead: the path went on and on, always the same and always rising. It was not very exciting.

"Come on, Badge! I wonder where we're getting to?"

He went on. After a time the slope grew even steeper, the rough stone floor breaking into ledges like a series of steps. He paused again, throwing the friendly golden light as far as it would reach. "I reckon we've come far enough, Bron. It goes on just the same, on'y more of a climb."

Sheppie pushed past and started to climb the first ledge. Bron followed, saying, "Oo, we got to see what's on top, here. Don't you want to, Badge?"

Of course he wanted to, and if it had been Sam——! But catching sight of her eager face he knew in a flash that even Sam would not have been a more willing companion than this new, changed Bron.

They climbed a long way, resting at intervals. Once a

bat dashed out: Bron only said, "Lucky I had me hair cut, for they say bats get tangled up in hair."

Sheppie was finding velvet mosses and tiny ferns, each more lovely than the last. They clung to wet cracks in the walls, for the tunnel had become a cleft without a roof: far, far above them they could catch a glimpse of the sky.

Soon, without warning, the path ceased rising and became level; there were queer black holes on either side and the air smelled different. Badge looked at the lamp, it seemed to have paled suddenly. "Come on," he muttered, "it's daylight! I reckon this is the end."

He grabbed Sheppie's hand and hurried on. Rounding a bend, they walked into an open space before a deep gully, and stood in daylight. "Wow!" he breathed, looking over the edge into a sickening black depth which the lantern's rays could not reach.

As he set the unwanted lantern on the ground he looked round. They were in a gloomy sort of daylight, very different from sweet sunshine; holes and shadows were everywhere and water dripped mournfully somewhere in the gully, while the humid air smelled of mildew and decay.

"Know what?" he whispered (though why he had to whisper he could not have said). "This is the crack in Devils' Hill, what Sam saw from the other side. 'Member, Bron?"

She nodded, staring up at the crack beyond the gully, which sloped between two crags till it reached the top. It ended in an arch of stone which caught the sunshine up there on a bar of gold.

"But this is the end," she sighed, studying the head of the awful gully, with nothing but a thread—a perilous, narrow thread—to serve as a track wriggling past it. "Ough, what a place to fall down!"

While they looked, and Bron tried not to shudder, they heard Sheppie behind say coaxingly, "Dog. Sheppie want. Want dog!"

Turning idly, to find out what new nonsense this was, both Badge and Bron saw at the same instant her "dog"— and the sight was so astonishing that even Badge lost the power to move. For her "dog" was a Tasmanian devil, fiercely alert and black as the gully beneath them. It had stopped a few steps short of Sheppie and they could see its mate close behind, in the tunnel they had just left.

For about as long as a drop of water takes to fall they all stared—Badge, Bron and Sheppie and the pair of devils simply stared at each other.

Badge gazed at the ugly head, forgetting to be afraid of the powerful jaws in his great interest; he noticed the dull black eyes, the hideous wide ears like flaps of pinkish membrane, the coarse hairs and the white patch on the chest like a crescent moon. He was seeing a devil close, in daylight and on its own ground! He almost loved it, he was so pleased.

But Bron's eyes, looking through glasses of fear, saw an enormous savage beast with terrible teeth making ready to tear them all to pieces—or at least force them to step back and fall down the bottomless gully. Too appalled even to shriek, her game little heart was nevertheless filled with one resolve—*it should not get Sheppie!*

Who can say what Sheppie saw? An animal the size of a terrier which must be a new kind of friendly dog? A huge new Ticcy? Perhaps just a fresh living thing in a world of endless new discovery. Fearlessly she stretched a hand to know it better by touching.

As for the devils, no one can guess what went on behind their wild, black eyes. No doubt they had the usual curiosity of bush creatures, and would have liked to follow these strange, queer-scented, two-legged animals farther. But Sheppie's outstretched hand was too alarming; the male sprang round amazingly fast for such a clumsy-looking brute—they had a glimpse of a white spot in the black fur above the tail and . . . that was all they saw.

The two devils had vanished. They *were* there—and now they were not there. It was as if the solid stone had opened a mouth and swallowed them both.

"*Oooo!*" came Bron's long-delayed shriek at last, as she made a grab at Sheppie. "Ooom—oom—mmm" boomed the echoes round the tunnel walls.

There was another sound—the clatter of the lantern

she knocked over in her haste. It crashed into the gully, bounced with a tinkling of smashed glass from rock to rock, till the sounds grew faint and were heard no more.

"Aw . . . what'll Dad say?" Badge gasped. "His big lantern! And he don't even know we took it!"

"I was that skerred I couldn't help," sobbed Bron. "When I set eyes on that thing . . . I . . . I . . ."

"Aw, well . . . he's still got the little lantern." Badge offered the only tiny crumb of comfort he could find. For the situation was terrible. Why had he come? Was this looking after the camp and the two nippers?

"I best count our matches, now we've no light to get us back," he mumbled, fumbling in his pocket.

"*No!*" Bron shrieked again. "I couldn't go back, Badge! Not if you paid me hundreds and thousands of pounds!"

She looked round wildly for means of escape, gazed fearfully at the awesome gully and the thread of a track past the top of it, then at the golden sunshine high up above and the blue sky showing through a gleaming arch. "Come on, Sheppie, we'll go and find Liddle-ma," she cried, snatching her firmly.

By the time Badge had grasped what she was doing, they had passed the worst bit and were climbing boulders the other side of the evil gully. "Come on, Badge"—there was a strange ring in Bron's voice now—"it's not too bad. Will I leave Sheppie and come back and help you?"

"No, hang on to her!" he shouted. This would be worse than crossing the Wire with the Gordon in flood, but Bron mustn't know how sick he felt. If he didn't look down . . . ? Come on, Badge, *get going,* he told himself.

He was over! He didn't need Bron's outstretched hand: he could sit on a boulder as though thinking out plans and give his trembling knees time to grow calm and still.

"But see, Bron, what'll we do if we don't find Dad and Liddle-ma on top?"

"Oo, Badge, you'll get us back. You'll find the way down into Sunset Valley," she told him with confidence, restored again to the old dependent Bron.

So of course he became confident himself—he had to be. "Thass right, Bron, we'll get down all right; but first we got to climb up where the crack starts, up under that arch."

Bron looked back at the gully and shuddered, "Oo, I never want to see this place again. Come on, Sheppie, you can play in the sunshine up there."

The climb was not difficult till the end, when they saw they must surmount a ridge and crawl through the golden archway over a mound of deep, loose sand.

Sheppie managed best. They pushed her in front and she was light enough to scramble quickly across, without sinking deeply. She vanished down the slope in the shadow of the broad archway while the other two were still hauling themselves up like mountain climbers through a snowdrift.

Sheppie had flung herself over like a parcel being sorted at a post office; and they could hear her now, the other side, making funny little snorts of joy and talking to something.

"Quick! What's she found now?" Bron, struggling along with the help of arms as well as legs, paused to look anxiously at Badge.

"Aw . . . a rock wallaby snoozing in the shade under the arch there? I can't hurry, Bron, me boots are full o' sand."

"But you know what she is!"

He hauled his legs onwards by a great effort, each one

feeling loaded with as much as Prince would carry on his back. He knew . . . Oh, he didn't doubt Sheppie had found something dangerous to play with, only why did he have to be the one left in charge of her?

Wading in the silent sand they heard a noise which seemed to crack the peace of the bush like a hammer blow. It began as a rumble and ended as a harsh bellow —the bellow of an anxious cow. The sound boomed past them and echoed down the gully, dying away between the walls of the tunnel.

"Brindle!" cried Badge, as understanding dawned.

"Sheppie!" shrieked Bron, whirling the sand round in her panic, and they both battled over the top at last.

Beneath the arch the land sloped to a distant rocky hollow, filled with reeds: it was up this incline that a cow came charging—running a few paces, stopping to listen, then charging on again.

For something had called the cow, something sleek and black and not a day old—something being clutched and hugged in the arms of the beaming Sheppie.

As Badge and Bron appeared it raised its head from her lap with another sad little "merrough—moo!"

"She's had a calf—a calf!" gulped Badge, his eyes glistening with wonder and joy. "Brindle's had a calf, an' Sheppie's found it!"

Then everything happened at once: as they charged down to Sheppie, the cow galloped up the slope to protect her young; and from somewhere out of sight, away to the south, came a great shout from Dad.

19

The Capture

S AM had lost all his jauntiness by the time he had struggled to the top of Devils' Hill. They had not found
Brindle's track at first, only the fearsome obstacle of a
forest of horizontal.

Horizontal is wicked stuff to bushmen; it grows like
a simple sapling to a certain height, then bends over and
lies horizontal with the ground, sending up a row of other
stems from this one trunk. In time these also bend over and
do the same thing, till in some Tasmanian forests you can
walk forty feet above ground, on a network of stems.

Dad wasted time skirting round this, and they had a

very rough climb up the crags of Devils' Hill till they struck a track that was clearly used by a cow. They followed its easy grade up the southern side, discovering that what appeared as an independent hill was really part of a long range which butted into Sunset Valley.

"Now what could fetch the old cow up here?" Dad mused. "Dry rock and no grass—and all that feed in the valley down below?"

Sam had no ideas to offer—or at least no breath to speak them. He rested thankfully on a big rock and wished his uncle wouldn't walk so fast.

"Maybe," Liddle-ma suggested, "it's more healthy-like? Up here there's no pests, no snakes—nothing to fear. And good, wholesome air, I reckon, without mists at night?"

"Could be she comes up just to sleep—too right, it could, mate. But then we've lost her, for she won't be here now."

Gloomily, Dad moved up the last bit and came out through a narrow cleft on to flat, rocky ground. On this side it was not bare rock, however; stunted scrub of gum and ti-tree made it difficult to see ahead, and there were dips and hollows as well as enough knobby outcrops of rock to hide a whole herd of cattle.

"You can take a spell, son," he told Sam, trudging wearily behind. "If we rousts her out she'll head back here and all you got to do is turn her again—and see she don't get past you."

So Sam was left.

He settled down in the shade of a straggly she-oak, having first had a bite to eat and a long pull at the cold tea bottle. No sound came from Dad and Liddle-ma who still hoped to come on the cow unawares and were working over the ground like a couple of bloodhounds.

Hours seemed to pass with nothing happening except an eagle's hovering, as it swooped low to take a look at him. It had been glorious at first, being the only idle one, but Sam was not used to being on his own and he was growing restive. Besides, he did not fancy the part they gave him. Waving a stick and yelling was not like dropping a noose of rope over a cow's horns and shouting, "Got her!"

He walked round, noting a knob of rock which would have been just the place to stand and throw—catching her in the narrow bit where the track went down—if only they had had the sense to leave the second rope with him . . . but they hadn't.

Sam sat down again. Then he got up hurriedly because of bull ants. He walked in a new direction and waited to listen; the clouds in the sky hardly moved and it was all very warm and still.

And *dull!* Why, he'd almost have had more fun staying in the cavern with Badge, he told himself bitterly. Poor old Badge was a bit of a hill-billy, as Mum said, but he wasn't so bad when you got to know him. Why, he'd be quite happy messing in the cave with the kids for he'd never been to the pictures and you couldn't see *him* trying to lasso a cow . . . well, *could* you! . . . but——

"Sam!"

There was Liddle-ma, beckoning through the trees only a few yards away.

"Sam, you can climb that big rock, that hillock over there, when I've gone," she whispered, pointing to the knobby tor in the distance. "Uncle Dave's seen her, she's having a drink down in a bit of a hollow there."

"Good-oh! Look, can I——"

"Shush!" she checked him. "We're closing in on her.

You climb up there and watch. If she breaks through, you bolt back here and turn her, see?"

Liddle-ma was gone and Sam began climbing his hillock. Eagerly he pushed his way to the top and then looked down. At a glance he saw the whole end of the hill, a half circle of crags sticking up like teeth, with—just opposite— one like an arch. The middle space was low and reedy, and there, sure enough, was a reddish brindle cow.

But she was not drinking, nor was she grazing; she was staring up the slope and bellowing. Why should she bellow? Surely she couldn't see Liddle-ma creeping towards that arch, rope in hand?

Sam was confused by other noises, too. Dad gave a great shout from somewhere, just as the cow charged up the slope towards Liddle-ma. Yet the cow stopped dead in front of the hole beneath the arch, and Liddle-ma was safe enough—she was hidden from sight at the back somewhere. It was strange.

Then Dad appeared below and Sam turned to watch him; he was running through the reeds where the cow had been, a rope looped ready in his hand. She heard him coming, however, and swung round to watch, too. Sam judged she was ready to break for the valley. He looked back, measuring the distance he would have to spring to stop her.

When he looked round again, Dad was standing like a gum tree in the reeds, and Brindle, reassured, was right up to the arch and lowing as if calling to something within.

But on top of that span of stone, wriggling towards her —and here Sam knew the whole thing must be some mad dream—*was Badge!*

Badge (who was really, of course, in the cavern waiting for their return) *appeared* to be lying on the arch of stone neatly dropping a noose of rope over Brindle's horns . . .

He'd done it!

She pulled back and whisked the rope from his hands of course—or else she would have dragged him down—but the rope was tight where it should be . . .

Gee! And good old Auntie had flung herself on the loose end, and was lying full stretch on the ground—on all those sharp stones, too!—holding it there . . . grabbing it . . .

Whee-oo! Would the old cow gore her? But Dad was attacking from behind; old Brindle didn't know which to charge first . . . Gee!

And now Dad's lasso was round her horns as well, and —and Sam, he didn't have to wait here any longer, did he? No!

"Good on yer!" he yelled, waving wildly to Badge. "Good on yer, Badge!"

Badge heard at last and waved back as he started to wriggle to the ground. There were yells from below the arch, too; Sam, as he raced along, even thought he heard a yelp of joy that could only have been made by Bron.

Dad tied the ropes to two trees and left Brindle to thresh about between them. "She'll dance a jig and bellow her head off till she gets used to it. Leave her be. I want to take a captain cook at what Sheppie's found," and he swung the delighted Sheppie on to his shoulders.

They were mad—mad with joy, mad as a snake—the whole lot of them!

Liddle-ma was laughing with tears rolling down her cheeks and rubbing the sore places where she fell; the boys were yelling and biffing each other; Bron screaming questions which no one answered, and Sheppie tugging

at Dad's gray hair as he danced her along towards her find.

"We got her!" Dad shouted the news to the great, wide, uncaring bush, "we got the cow, we got the calf!" He broke into lusty song:

"Shearing is all over and we've got our check,
Up with our swags and off on the trek.
The first pub we come to we're going to have a
spree . . ."

But they broke in before he ever reached the chorus with their loud,

"Click go the shears, boys,
Click—click—click!"

never stopping till they stood before the arch.

"Merrough-merr!" grumbled the little black calf all wobbly on its very new legs. Somehow, it felt sure these animals were not the mother it could hear calling in the distance.

They stood round at last in silence, watching Dad examine it. "A fine little heifer, born last night—when we heard Brindle," he said.

"Thass right," Badge pointed to the back of the arch. "The noise goes back down there to the gully——" he stopped short.

"What's the matter? What's up, son?"

"Dad, I busted the big hurricane, down there."

"No, you never!" protested Bron in a shrill squeak. "I sort of kicked it. I couldn't help, I——"

"That's enough!" boomed Dad. "At the moment I couldn't care less about what you broke." But then he thought a moment and added, "I hope it was on'y the glass?"

"No," Badge mumbled miserably, "it was the whole bag o' tricks went over the edge."

"Accidents," Liddle-ma said as she always did, "happen in the best families. What's done, 's done."

"You still got the little one," Badge reminded Dad gently.

"Well, don't bust that. Not without you rope me another cow," Dad grinned, and everyone laughed and talked at once, and asked questions—till Liddle-ma shoo'd them out because they were terrifying the calf.

They sat in the sunshine across the entrance, where they could guard their little black prisoner, while Liddle-ma produced food from her bag. Gradually the questions were answered.

"Me?" said Sam. "I saw it all from up the dress circle. Nearly toppled down with shock when old Badge crawls on the arch, here, and throws a lasso. Wish I'd been him!"

Dad looked at him curiously for a moment. "Don't worry, Sam, his mum couldn't have give him the rope to throw if you hadn't waited where you was told—she'd have been back where you was, keeping guard. Good on yer, son."

"Too right, I would! You did well, Sam. And so did Bron and Sheppie, holding that calf so it wouldn't clear off to Brindle." Liddle-ma wrapped them in her warm smile. "There was our Bron, brave as a lion, hanging on to one leg while Sheppie hangs round its neck, and old Brindle ramping up as though she'd stick a horn through them."

"Good kids, the lot of you." Dad paused for a long drink from the tea bottle. "Butter on your bread and cream on your porridge!—when we gets this lot home, I mean."

129

He went off singing:

"With me little white flour bag a-sitting on the
  stump,
Me little tea and sugar bag looking nice and
  plump,
A little fat cod fish just off the hook,
And four little johnny cakes a *credit to the cook!*"

20

Sheppie Names Her Find

B RINDLE was less frantic, did not strain so hard against the branch which she supposed had caught her horns, though she still plunged wildly when she saw her calf in Dad's arms.

He placed its ridiculous legs on the ground while she bellowed motherly endearments. The calf stared, answered with a slobbery "Merrr-rr," and rushed at her with waving tail.

They stood watching its eager sucking, and the tender way Brindle licked it with her great rough tongue till she could reach no farther because of the rope.

"Dad, I just don't get it," Badge sighed, after giving some problem deep thought. "Where's the bull?"

"Quite right, son—it got me beat at first, finding on'y part o' the family, like. But then I noticed the calf's color, and thought o' the time your Uncle Link said there was a black bullock wild in the bush, if it wasn't dead. I thought about it when I come on some tracks down in the valley, but like a silly gallah I never thought o' *this*," and he nodded happily at the busy calf.

"What are you going to call her?" Liddle-ma asked Sheppie.

This was a grave matter and Sheppie seemed to have no ideas, so everyone made suggestions for her. Velvet, Blackie, Smoky and Shadow—to each she shook her head.

"Well, go on, you say!"

Sheppie looked at Liddle-ma and made a small "Merr-rr" sound, like the calf.

"That's it," said Liddle-ma, understanding at once. "I knew a girl called that; it's a nice name—Merle."

So Sheppie's calf was Merle.

Dad glanced at the sun and looked over his troops, saying briskly, "She's had her drink, Merle has, and we must get going. Sam! You know the track, you and Badge take turns carrying Merle in front, so's Brindle will want to follow. Me and Liddle-ma'll hang on to a rope each side, to see she don't run you down. Bron? Bron's got a big job. You got to take a stick and get her going if she stops; Bron . . ." he paused uncertainly, "there's Sheppie, too?"

"Oo, we'll be right, won't we, Sheppie?" Bron promised valiantly, though she added quickly, "On'y don't go too fast, will you, Uncle Dave?"

At first it was not a success.

Merle, full of milk and sleepy, got tired of answering the "lost child" hullabaloo behind her and Brindle suddenly decided she must have left her behind. Like a mother who remembers her child abandoned in a shop, she swung about—and it took all Dad's strength to prevent her trampling over Bron and Sheppie, who followed too close behind.

After that they had to come close and let her actually sniff Merle, before she would move on again in the right direction. As it was, she kept returning to this great idea of a calf behind her, till Dad said, "Me arms are fair tore out o' their sockets, trying to hold the flaming cow."

"Oo, you mustn't call her that, Unk, now she's got a calf," Bron reproved him, while they had a few minutes' rest.

"No? Well, Bron, you think o' a way to get her along and I'll call her me bronze-wing pigeon if you like."

"If Badge and me and Sheppie goes in front, and Sam drives her along?"

"H'mn . . . Bron's said something."

It worked—though progress was slow. At every turn, Badge would wait while Dad hitched his rope to a tree or a rock, everyone resting till he had made certain they were on the right track.

So they struggled down the steepest part of the hill.

Then, Dad had a better idea; he tied both ropes into one long one, set the calf on the ground to run to her mother, and drove the two gently forward. Brindle could fancy herself free—till she tried to run away: then they all helped Dad battle with her on the rope, and she learned sense.

At last they had skirted the forest of horizontal, keeping to Brindle's own excellent track, and were close above Sunset Valley; and as it happened, the sun was even then making ready to dip behind a blue-black line of mountain and cloud, filling their valley with a fiery glory.

"Whoa, mare!" Dad shouted, hitching the rope to a tree. They left the weary Brindle peacefully licking Merle, and stood gazing down, picking out landmarks. Dad wanted to know about the tunnel, and "Sam's Crack" which ended at the Arch on top, but there was nothing of this to be seen from where they stood.

133

"It's a queer valley," Liddle-ma nodded thoughtfully.
"I never seen its like . . . the color down there now!"

"And the birds . . . and the flowers on the trees!"

"Thass right, son, and the green; and the lovely little
pools. But there's bad there, too. Snakes . . . that great
gray mist!"

"Oo, and the devils in the hill," Bron added with relish.

But Badge wouldn't have that. "We was devils to them, Bron. They was here first, see? Minding their own business, they was, when we come along. Aw, I reckon they thought us devils."

"Take your last eyeful o' Sunset Valley at sunset. We

can't eat it, and I want my tucker," Dad proclaimed.

That made everyone say they could eat a house, or an elephant, or anything at all except what Liddle-ma promised on their return—pea soup.

"It's a bit o' a birthday, like," Dad suggested, "Merle's birthday. Nearly one day old. No candle?—no cake?"

"All right," she had to laugh, "no soup, no peas. We'll open the reserve tins for the last night in Sunset Cavern."

By the time they had Brindle and Merle safely fixed within reach of water, and the horses collected and fed, they were tired out. Bron had gone ahead with Sheppie, and the youngest pioneer was already asleep when the boys climbed wearily into the cavern. But Bron had the billy boiling and Liddle-ma was opening bully beef.

Badge and Bron had made a plan to lead the rest a little way along the tunnel after tea—Sam having enviously bet Bron she hadn't really seen a devil, and Badge betting Sam he could show him one—but as they munched and stuffed sitting in the warmth of the fire they grew so sleepy it became an effort even to eat.

In fact, Badge was sure he *had* led them through a long tunnel in a gray mist and without a light; he saw without surprise Sheppie patting a man-size Tasmanian devil and feeding it with bits of bully beef. Only Sheppie was somehow Merle.

Then, he knew it was a dream and tried to go on dreaming it; but Dad was shaking him by the shoulder. "Come on, son. Got to rise and shine. All set for another hot day and we got to push that flaming cow across the valley."

21

Sam the Boss

Food was the trouble.

"Porridge and honey for breakfast. Stuff in all you can eat for there's nothing more," said Liddle-ma with great cheerfulness.

"No bread?"

"No bread or damper. Be glad o' something hot today, for there won't be that at the next camp, Dad says. He reckons it won't be safe to light another fire, or we'll have the bush a-blaze."

Badge cleared his mouth from the stuffing operation, resting his spoon to remark, "Good job Sam found us this place to camp, weren't it, Liddle-ma?"

Sam looked modestly at his bowl, ears alert; but Liddle-ma continued without so much as a glance his way. "Dad's gone on; he's getting Brindle and Merle across the valley by stages, so they can rest up in the heat o' the day. You boys are to hurry after him with Prince and Di'mond."

"Can I ride Narrups?"

"No, Sam. The pony waits till the end, after Bron has helped me turn the last of the flour into loaves, which we'll bake in the ashes before the fire goes out."

So, when they couldn't manage one lick more, they fetched the loaded horses. Sam went proudly on ahead, leading Prince (though of course it was really Prince leading Sam, for that wise old horse knew just where Dad was and all about turning for home) while Badge followed with Diamond ambling behind him.

Sunset Valley was just as lovely at daybreak as at the glorious folding up of the light, but Badge hardly noticed the freshness and the bird song, the golden whistler that kept them company or the dewy patch of orchids which Diamond blundered through. He was thinking. He was wondering. Didn't Liddle-ma *like* Sam? There was something in her voice when she spoke to him . . . something not there when she spoke to Bron. But Dad liked him—now. You could tell that by the jobs he gave him to do.

Liddle-ma raked a crusty flat loaf from the hot gray ashes, dusted it, and turned it on its back in front of Bron. "Tap it with your knuckles—like this, see? If it sounds hollow, then it's done. Is that the last one?"

"Yes, Auntie."

"Whiles it cools we'll fix the load on the pony and bring back some water for the fire. My word, you look hot, Bron! Like a dip in the pool to cool off?"

At first Bron thought she wouldn't, but when she got there and knew Liddle-ma was standing, big and strong, to defend her against snakes and other terrors, she changed her mind. So she and Sheppie peeled off the little they wore and had a glorious cool-off. Of course they got hot again walking back, but it didn't matter.

"If them boys have any sense, they'll be doing the same and having a swim up the top end," Liddle-ma said as she put down her bucket of water on the cool floor of the cavern. She was just going to tip the contents on the fire when there came a shout from outside.

"It's Sam and Badge—they got something," Bron cried.

"Hey, Auntie! Don't put the fire out!" Sam yelled.

"Look what Sam's caught!" Badge shouted, holding up to her gaze Dad's largest billy full of ugly green claws and a scaly body. "A beaut crayfish!"

"*Well!*" She leaned over the edge to see better. "Just what the doctor ordered, Sam! Bring it up and I'll cook it at once."

But he still stood there, showing his capture to the awed gaze of Bron who stared from above, explaining how he scooped it out of the water when Dad sent them for a swim. "It's not a yabbi, Bron. It's a cray all right—look!"

There is a difference between lobsters and crayfish of the sea and their fresh-water relations of the creeks, but between the latter and the little yabbis children love to catch is only a difference of size. Sam's was certainly a "cray"—with about enough meat to give each one a good bite.

As Liddle-ma made these calculations she saw Sam nudge Badge; they grinned at each other and broke into their own version of "Johnny Cakes," which ended:

"A big fat crayfish just off the hook,
  And lots of Auntie's soda bread *a credit to the
    cook!*"

"You beggars! I see I got to pay for it," she laughed,
and went to pick out the smallest loaf to throw down to
them.

They left the cavern when all sensible wild creatures
were resting in the midday heat, for the valley was hot
as an oven. Twice they disturbed wallaby sleeping in the
scrub, and Brindle—when Liddle-ma's party at last joined
Dad's—was giving trouble. In fact she had decided on
a sit-down strike.

They sat beside her on a shady slope, tearing delicious
morsels of "cray" from the shell to make the feast of plain
bread more interesting. Soon they followed the example
of the tired little calf, even Dad closing his eyes.

All the afternoon they struggled up the long incline
towards the Look-out without reaching it. Brindle was, as
Dad put it, "playing up a treat." It was not till the sun
was tumbling to the western hills that she became a little
manageable, after they discovered she would follow behind
Prince.

"Now why won't that flaming cow follow Di'mond?"
Dad asked, exasperated.

"I reckon," Badge brought out slowly, "it's because of
Prince being black. See, Merle's dad's black, isn't he?"

"By crumbs, the boy's said something! She's used to
trotting behind a big black rump." Dad shook Badge in
mock anger. "Why couldn't you have thought that up before, son?"

"Oo, Badge, you are clever," murmured Bron admiringly, and he couldn't prevent his face glowing like the sunset.

But Brindle had stopped again, on an outcrop nowhere in particular.

"We can't camp here, and it'll be dark soon," Liddle-ma reminded Dad.

"I know. I been thinking. You push on, mate, with the pack horses, and leave me with the cow. One o' the boys'll take my place and fix a shelter and make a camp as soon as he finds you a good spot. Which one . . . ? Well, both could do it, but I'd say *Sam*. He's the man for the job, I reckon. Will we make him camp boss?"

"What about Badge?"

"Give Badge my old bluey; him and me will roll up near the flaming cow and push her along, bit by bit, as soon as it's light."

"Oo—Sam the Boss!" Bron made a face at him, but it was quite a friendly face. She looked dismayed when he got up at once and walked towards some gum trees, without saying a word to Dad or anyone. Dad didn't seem to mind, he was smiling after him, but Badge called quickly, "Where you going, Sam?"

"Get some peppermint leaves . . . fresh ones . . . Ticcy," was the terse answer jerked out by the usually long-winded Sam. Was he copying Badge?

It was a still, bright night and Sam's camp was in a good spot; no one woke through rolling down a slope or because of sharp things sticking into tender parts of the body, though once they were all disturbed by the mating cries of a pair of possums overhead.

Badge did not fare so well, for Dad used the warm, clear hours of night and early morning to urge Brindle forward in several short pushes, leaving him to carry Merle. They reached Sam's camp just as breakfast was being handed round. It was cold potatoes which had been baked in their skins, eaten with beef dripping or honey. Nothing else.

"One thing," said Bron, gnawing cheerfully into hers, "there won't be any washing-up!"

The day was as hot as ever. Dad hardly dared light his pipe now, for fear of starting a bush fire. Liddle-ma kept staring anxiously in the direction of home, wondering if all was well there; and whether her garden was dying of drought, or the ravages of wild creatures from the bush.

They could not hurry, because Dad would not hustle Brindle in the heat of the day, though she followed Prince quite well now. He said it would be bad for her to hurry; she would have no milk for the calf. Even Ticcy wanted only to sleep in the shade.

Somehow, with their golden Sunset Valley lost to sight behind the hills, they were all in a fever to reach home. It was maddening to move as fitfully as a spider. Somehow, too, the talk was all of food; all they would eat when they got the chance.

"Gee, I'd like a great big steak as thick as a fence post," said Sam, "—no, I wouldn't! I'll have six helpings of roast goose and green peas."

"Six goes? There won't be much left for us!"

"Yeah, there'll be lots, if it's one like the big goose my Dad's saving for Christmas. And fruit salad after, with quarts of thick cream."

"You didn't mention potatoes, son?" Liddle-ma looked at him with a sly twinkle, and they hooted when Sam made a comic face and said fervently, "No, thanks, Auntie! *No spuds!*"

142

It was dark when they reached the great fallen tree of their first camp and rolled under it to sleep. They were such hardened campers they did not bother to unfasten and put up the tarpaulin, this time.

"What's that white thing up the far end?" Dad asked as he flashed the small lantern round.

Badge crawled to examine it and held up a scrap of white cotton, all that was left of a bag of flour.

"Well, we've given something a free feed," he grinned.

22

Cobbers

THERE being no temptation to linger over a scanty breakfast, the procession was soon on its homeward way; and now the hills showed familiar faces and the ranges could be recognized.

"There's Three Fists over there to the north," Dad said, pointing. "Soon, I reckon, we'll get a glimpse o' the valley; and Liddle-ma—if so be as she's got the eye of a n'awk?—she'll be able to tell if there's any termarters left for Sam in the garden."

They reached the spot he had in mind in the early

144

afternoon. There was no view of the floor of the valley because of dense trees on the ridge, but it was their valley all right. Dad saw something, too, which made him whistle.

"Yes," Liddle-ma agreed, following his eyes, "that's smoke. I've thought I smelled it once or twicc today. Sam! . . . Where's Sam? Oh, why didn't I go back and see to that fire meself!"

Dad had hurried away: there was only Bron to hear her bitter self-reproaches. "Why did I trust that boy to douse the fire. I been worried every day this would happen —all because I didn't turn back."

"Will I go and ask Sam again, Auntie?"

"No, no! What's done's done—and I'm to blame. We'll soon know . . . if we get going quick."

They hustled poor Brindle at last, promising her a life of ease ever after in a beautiful paddock with meals fetched to her twice a day—if only she would hurry along now.

Brindle hurried.

Once inside the paddock Dad removed the rope from her horns. From the slip-rails they all watched for a minute to see what she would do—expecting anything. But the mettlesome Brindle merely stood in a shady place with heaving flanks.

Worried as she was, Liddle-ma watched with satisfaction. "We got a beaut little cow in Old Bow'ra's calf. Look at her now!" Brindle was standing tenderly licking Merle all over.

"Aw, yeah!" Badge beamed from the top rail. "She knows she's home. Look at 'em now, Sheppie! Can you see——? Hey!" he broke off abruptly, "where is she? *Where's Sheppie?*"

145

At this the whole line leaning on the rails or hanging over the fence turned about and Dad let out a mighty shout: *"Good on yer, Link!"*

For Sheppie was belting down the track as fast as she could go, straight into her father's arms.

"Mean to tell me it was you made all that smoke, Link?" Liddle-ma wondered, as her eyes swept the beloved valley and the blue haze in the small gullies round it.

But she could not get his immediate attention, he was happily telling them his news all over again with twiddles and extras.

"I tell you, Sam, your Mum's like a kookaburra what's swallered a snake; she's like a day old chick; she's prancing round like an emu ever since she got back from that old hospital. Like a bunch o' boronia she is, all sweet with joy o' being home again."

"My word, Link," Dad smote him on the shoulder, "you must be thankful."

"I'll say I'm thankful," said his brother simply.

"So you left her and the twins, with old Ruby Bunton to look after them, and came to tell your nippers? And found us all cleared off like a rainy day!"

"I come to fetch 'em home, Dave, knowing how short you was of tucker—with Ole Bow'ra gone, and that."

At this they all started to tell him at once—so that he said he couldn't hear a thing—and Sheppie seized him by the hand and dragged him towards the paddock, where the sight of Brindle explained a lot. Dad added details.

"By c-cucumber! You fetched in the one that got away? —and she's had a calf, so there'll soon be milk for you again? Aw, feed it to me slow, it's too much for an old man to take in all at once," declared Uncle Link in tones which made each one grow at least an inch taller in a minute. "And *who* found her?"

"Sheppie did!"

"*Sheppie?* Well, nothing surprises me any more," he stated with an enormous wink in her direction, "not even the fact that I've seen her face at last, without hair all over her eyes. Come to that, what's Bron done to herself? She looks diff'rent."

Badge's eyes twinkled as he imitated the casual manner. "Aw, Bron's seen a couple o' devils in a sort o' cave she wanted to look in, Unk; maybe——"

"Bron digging out wild devils? Draw it mild, son! Draw it mild!"

"Thass right, Link," Liddle-ma smiled, "but give us a

147

go, do! I'm trying to ask about all the smoke in the valley? Was the fire right out when you——"

"Fire out?" he interrupted. "I never set eyes on one *outer!* Some gallah must've tipped a tank o' water on the hot ashes so they set like a cake, and when I come to get her going——"

But Liddle-ma checked him with a quick gesture which brought a sudden silence. "Now listen," she said, "I got to tell Sam I'm sorry for thinking he didn't do the job proper, which he did. I got worrying about a bush fire starting——"

"Aw, Sam understands—don't you, Sam?" Dad put in rapidly, and while he smiled at his aunt Dad went on, "Sam's not a kid any more. Night before last he made the camp and took charge for his Auntie, whiles Badge and me fetched along that flaming cow, Link."

"Well," said his father in a tone that was almost hushed, and stared at his son's shorn head, "if that don't beat all! Sam's lost his curls and Sam's made a camp. Soots me, but what will his Mum say?"

"Cut it out, Dad!" muttered his son uncomfortably. "Did you bring along a bit to eat?"

"Fair broke me back humping you in a feast for to-night."

There was a sound like a dying wind, a wave breaking on shingles, or hungry people sighing with content at the prospect of food.

"Oo! What did you bring us, Dad?"

"It's in the iron pot now; you'll soon know, Bron."

And so, once they had rested a little and gloated with Uncle Link over Brindle and her calf, they left the slip rails and swung on towards home like a pack of kangaroo dogs, nose down on a scent.

148

It was a glorious feast and when Uncle Link looked round there remained only a pile of clean-picked bones on a tin plate in the middle of the table.

"That was the biggest goose on the farm. I reckoned it would go a couple o' meals or more, but it slipped down easy in one, seeing I cooked it a treat. I'm a good cook," said he modestly, and no one liked to tell him they could almost have eaten it raw, so ravenous were they feeling.

"You cooked it perfect," said Liddle-ma, "and the butter's welcome, too. It'll keep us going till Brindle's milk comes up and we can take the calf from her."

"Yeah, you should be set now—once I take Sam and the girls off tomorrow."

"And Badge? Won't Badge come too?" cried Bron in dismay.

"Badge'll be along in a week's time, at the full o' the moon. He don't have to come before, on account o' school not starting till then."

Sam put down his spoon with a bang. "Then why do I have to go home?" he demanded. "Why can't I come along with Badge?"

There was a brief silence: eyes were staring at him curiously—but not those in Badge's flushed face because they were already fixed on his plate to hide a look of wonder.

Dad was scratching his chin and looking at his brother with a little smile. "We'll have him and welcome, won't we, Liddle-ma?"

"Too right, we will, Link!"

"Your Mum, she'll create . . ." Sam's father hesitated, seeming bewildered, then he asked, "Why d'you want to stay, son?"

"Well, see, Dad, there's things Badge and me got to do together. Can't Mum spare me the last week of holidays? Tell her she's got me all term time."

"That's so."

"Tell her, Dad"—he dropped his eyes, for now Badge was gazing straight at him—"tell her about Badge and me being cobbers."

"I will, son. I'm—I'm glad of it."

"Good on you, Dad!"

"Good on you, Sam!" He winked.

23

Badge Gets Going

SHOWERS on several days had broken the drought and
now the little breeze of early morning was cool and
fresh on Badge's cheek; to the east the sky rippled with
pink in what he and Iggy called "lolly clouds."

"Well, I best get going," he said, busy fixing the ropes
of his pack while his mother smiled as she watched him.

"Thass right, son. Sam's with Dad down the track putting the new box you made for Ticcy on top o' the load. My word, Sheppie will be pleased—I can just see her grinning over it. She was real set up when you gave her that possum to take away."

"We made something for Bron, too. Know what?"

"No, what is it, son?"

"A snake-skin belt, instead o' that silly bit o' red plastic one. It were Sam's idea. Mind you, the snake'll smell for a bit, but Sam reckons after she's wore it a time the smell will go."

"She'll think she's Christmas with that on, son. Oh, you won't forget to say they're both to come out here to our place for Christmas holidays, will you?"

He humped his load and looked up at her with a smile like the sun on a snow-field. "If I forget everything, Liddle-ma, I won't forget that! Sam and me, we been thinking what we'll do . . ." he turned his head and stared to the south in the direction of Devils' Hill.

Somewhere in the bush the mournful notes of a pallid cuckoo marked the passing of time. Badge remained heedless, staring over the ranges at something far away . . . dreaming . . . dreaming . . .

"Is he ready?" came a shout down the track.

"Good-oh, Dad! I'm coming!"

"Give Aunt Florrie a hand, won't you, son? Remember she's been sick."

"Yeah. Sam and me, we'll split the wood for her. He's taking her the yabbis he caught. See, he reckons they're *or*most as big as a cray."

She nodded, thinking they were *or*most as small as a tadpole. "She'll be pleased, Aunt Florrie will."

They exchanged a shy smile and he said again, "Well, I best get going, now," and turned about.

There was mud in all the pot-holes from the night's rain; his boots squished through it delightfully. He saw Sam ahead and started to hurry, for hadn't Sam said he had a green frog in his pocket to show him?